W9-BPL-925

Greek
Myths

Greek Myths

BY

Olivia E. Coolidge

ILLUSTRATED BY

Edouard Sandoz

HOUGHTON MIFFLIN COMPANY · BOSTON

Text copyright © 1949 by Olivia E. Coolidge
Copyright renewed © 1977 by Olivia E. Coolidge

All rights reserved. For information about permission to reproduce selections
from this book, write to Permissions, Houghton Mifflin Company,
215 Park Avenue South, New York, New York 10003.

HC ISBN 0-618-15425-6   PAP ISBN 0-618-15426-4

Library of Congress Cataloging-in-Publication Data is available for this title.

Printed in the United States of America

QUM 10 9 8 7 6 5 4 3 2 1

CONTENTS

A TABLE OF THE CHIEF GODS OF ANCIENT GREECE

OLDER GODS

Zeus *Latin, Jupiter.* King of Gods. Symbols: thunderbolt and eagle.

Hera *Latin, Juno.* Queen of Gods. Symbol: peacock.

Hades *Latin, Pluto.* God of underworld. Brother of Zeus.

Poseidon *Latin, Neptune.* God of sea. Brother of Zeus. Symbols: bull and trident.

Demeter *Latin, Ceres.* Goddess of grain. Mother of Persephone, *Latin, Proserpina.*

YOUNGER GODS

Aphrodite Also Cypris. *Latin, Venus.* Goddess of love and beauty. Symbols: the dove and the seagull. Born from the sea.

Apollo Also Phoebus Apollo. *Latin, Phoebus* or *Apollo.* God of the sun, god of prophecy, god of poetry and song. Symbols: golden chariot, golden lyre, golden bow and arrows, laurel.

Ares *Latin, Mars.* God of war.

Artemis *Latin, Diana.* Twin sister of Apollo. Goddess of the moon, huntress, goddess of unmarried girls. Symbols: silver chariot, silver bow and arrows.

Athene Also Pallas Athene. *Latin, Minerva, Athena.* Goddess of wisdom, goddess of household arts, a goddess of war. Symbols: owl, olive, Gorgon's head.

Dionysus *Latin, Bacchus.* God of wine, god of tragedy. Symbols: ivy, vine. Rites known as mysteries or orgies. Followers, Bacchantes.

Eros *Latin, Cupid.* Son of Aphrodite. God of love.

Hephaistos *Latin, Vulcan.* God of metalworkers and craftsmen. The lame god.

Hermes *Latin, Mercury.* Messenger of the Gods, god of thieves. Symbols: winged hat and sandals, staff with two snakes twined round it, called the caduceus.

MINOR GODS

Nymphs Woodland nymphs called **Dryads**, river nymphs, sea nymphs called **Nereids**, cloud nymphs.

Minor Olympians **Eos**, *Latin, Aurora,* goddess of dawn. **The Muses**, nine goddesses of poetry, history, music. **The Graces**. **Iris**, goddess of rainbow. **Hebe**, goddess of youth. **Ganymede**, cupbearer of Gods.

Sea Gods	**Nereus**, father of sea nymphs. **Proteus**, god who can change into many shapes. **Phorcys**, god of the sea beasts—seals, sea lions.
Woodland Gods	**Pan**, half goat, half man. God of herdsmen. Symbol: reed pipes. **The Satyrs**, goat-gods like **The Centaurs**, half horse, half man.
Sky Gods	**The Winds**, especially **Zephyr**, the warm, gentle west wind, and **Boreas**, the stormy north wind.
Underworld Gods	**Charon**, the ferryman over the river Styx.

INTRODUCTION

G reek legends have been favorite stories for many centuries. They are mentioned so often by famous writers that it has become impossible to read widely in English, or in many other literatures, without knowing what the best of these tales are about. Even though we no longer believe in the Greek gods, we enjoy hearing of them because they appeal to our imagination.

The Greeks thought all the forces of nature were spirits, so that the whole earth was filled with gods. Each river, each woodland, even each great tree had its own god or nymph. In the woods lived the satyrs, who had pointed ears and the shaggy legs of goats. In the sea danced more than three thousand green-haired, white-limbed maidens. In the air rode wind gods, cloud nymphs, and the golden chariot of the sun. All these spirits, like the forces of nature, were beautiful and strong, but sometimes unreliable and unfair. Above all, however, the Greeks felt that they were tremendously interested in mankind.

From very early times the Greeks began to invent stories to account for the things that went on—the change
of seasons, the sudden storms, the good and bad fortune of the farmer's year. These tales were spread by
travelers from one valley to another. They were put together and altered by poets and musicians, until at last
a great body of legends arose from the whole of Greece.
These did not agree with one another in details, but, on
the whole, gave a clear picture of who the chief gods
were, how men should behave to please them, and what
their relationships had been with heroes of the past.

The ruler of all the gods was Zeus, the sky god, ti-
tled by courtesy father of gods and men. He lived in the
clouds with most of the great gods in a palace on the
top of Mount Olympus, the tallest mountain in Greece.
Lightning was the weapon of Zeus, thunder was the
rolling of his chariot, and when he nodded his head, the
whole earth shook.

Zeus, though the ruler of the world, was not the eldest of the gods. First had come a race of monsters with
fifty heads and a hundred arms each. Next followed elder gods called Titans, the leader of whom, Kronos, had
reigned before Zeus. Then arose mighty giants, and finally Zeus and the Olympians. Zeus in a series of wars
succeeded in banishing the Titans and imprisoning the
giants in various ways. One huge monster, Typhon, lay
imprisoned under the volcano of Aetna, which spouted
fire when he struggled. Atlas, one of the giants, was
forced to stand holding the heavens on his shoulders so
that they should not fall upon the earth.

Almost as powerful as Zeus were his two brothers, who did not live on Olympus: Poseidon, ruler of the sea, and Hades, gloomy king of the underworld, where the spirits of the dead belong. Queen of the gods was blue-eyed, majestic Hera. Aphrodite, the laughing, sea-born goddess, was queen of love and most beautiful of all. Apollo and Artemis were twins, god of the sun and goddess of the moon. Apollo was the more important. Every day he rode the heavens in a golden chariot from dawn to sunset. The sun's rays could be gentle and healing, or they could be terrible. Apollo, therefore, was a great healer and the father of the god of medicine. At the same time he was a famous archer, and the arrows from his golden bow were arrows of infection and death. Apollo was also god of poetry and song; his instrument was a golden lyre, and the nine Muses, goddesses of music and the arts, were his attendants. He was the ideal of young manhood and the patron of athletes.

Apollo was also god of prophecy. There were temples of Apollo, known as oracles, at which a man could ask questions about the future. The priestesses of Apollo, inspired by the god, gave him an answer, often in the form of a riddle which was hard to understand. Nevertheless, the Greeks believed that if a man could interpret the words of the oracle, he would find the answer to his problem.

Artemis, the silver moon goddess, was goddess of unmarried girls and a huntress of wild beasts in the mountains. She also could send deadly arrows from her silver bow.

Grey-eyed Athene, the goddess of wisdom, was patron of Athens. She was queen of the domestic arts, particularly spinning and weaving. Athene was warlike too; she wore helmet and breastplate, and carried a spear. Ares, however, was the real god of war, and the maker of weapons was Hephaistos, the lame smith and metal worker.

One more god who lived on Olympus was Hermes, the messenger. He wore golden, winged sandals which carried him dry-shod over sea and land. He darted down from the peaks of Olympus like a kingfisher dropping to catch a fish, or came running down the sloping sunbeams bearing messages from Zeus to men. Mortal eyes were too weak to behold the dazzling beauty of the immortals; consequently the messages of Zeus usually came in dreams. Hermes was therefore also a god of sleep, and of thieves because they prowl by night. Healing was another of his powers. His rod, a staff entwined by two snakes, is commonly used as a symbol of medicine.

The Greeks have left us so many stories about their gods that it hardly would be possible for everyone to know them all. The following tales are some of the ones which have pleased the most people and been most widely used by dramatists and poets. We can still enjoy them because they are good stories. In spite of their great age we can still understand them because they are about nature and about people. We still need them to enrich our knowledge of our own language and of the great masterpieces of literature.

Greek Myths

I

STORIES OF THE GODS

The Trickery of Hermes

Hermes, god of thieves and messenger of Zeus, was full of trickery from the start. His mother, the shy nymph, Maia, bore him secretly in a deep cave, but since the baby god could walk and talk from his birth, she could not hide him long. In fact, when she laid him in the cradle and turned away to let him sleep, he slipped out behind her back and stole to the cave entrance with mischief in his mind. In the grass outside the gateway he found a great tortoise with a spotted shell and seized on it to play with. He took the shell and from it made a framework, stretching seven strings of sheep-gut upon it. Thus he constructed a new and beautiful instrument: a lyre, a kind of harp, and began to play. It sounded marvelous, and as he plucked the strings, he sang to it stories of his mother and of his father, Zeus, and of the cave where he was born and the nymphs that served them there.

Presently, when Hermes tired of his new toy, he laid it in his cradle and slipped forth again to get into some real mischief. Just as the sun was going down, he found a mountain side where a great herd of snow-white cattle grazed, the cattle of the sun. Fifty of these the baby god of thieves separated from the herd and began to drive away, down past the sandy river bed to the hard ground beyond, where it would be more difficult to trace their footprints. To make all safe, with much shouting and running, he turned the cattle and forced them to walk backwards through the sandy place so that Apollo might think they were coming to, not going from, their pasture. To conceal his own footprints from the god, he tied branches, leaves and all, under his feet, making great, shuffling tracks, as though someone had been sweeping the sand with a broom.

In spite of all his cunning he did not get away unseen, for an old man working in a vineyard looked up in wonder as the baby god came past. Hermes had his hands full at the time. He was hurrying to get the cattle away before the sun found out they were gone. Consequently he merely called out to the man and promised him good crops if he would keep silent. Then he raced off after the cattle, letting the old man think what he would.

Hermes drove the herd to a distant meadow by a river and penned them there. He killed two of them in sacrifice to the twelve great gods of Olympus, thinking perhaps that before very long he might be in trouble and need the Olympians' aid. Then he hurried back to his home, stole silently into the hall, and jumped into his cradle. There he covered himself up and tried to look like an innocent little baby, though with the left hand he still kept fingering his lyre beneath the clothes.

When the dawn came, Apollo rose, went to the mountainside as his custom was, and looked down on his cattle. Immediately he noticed the theft and called down to a poor old man who was driving his ox to pasture, asking if he had noticed anything.

"I was working in my vineyard yesterday," said the old man, "when I saw a strange sight. A little child, a baby, with a long staff in his hand was driving away a herd of cattle, running from side to side and forcing them to walk backwards with their heads toward him."

It is hard to conceal things from Apollo because he is the god of prophecy, and immediately he knew about Hermes and who he was, secret as his birth had been. As for tracing the cattle, that was a different matter. The tracks went not only backwards; they went up and down and from side to side, while over all were great sweeping marks. Further along, on the hard ground, there were simply no traces at all. Apollo gave up looking for them. Instead he made off for Maia's cave to confront the baby thief.

Hermes snuggled down inside the bedclothes when he saw Apollo coming, and he hunched himself together as best he could, trying to look very tiny indeed. This was hard for him, since he had grown considerably in his first day. He could not deceive Apollo, who came up to the cradle, demanding angrily, "Where are my cattle, you thief? Tell me at once what you have done with them, or I will cast you down into darkness forever, and you can see how you like thieving there."

Hermes peeped up at him over the edge of the bedclothes and said in a weak little voice, "Why are you shouting at me about cattle? I am just a poor little baby. The only things I care about are good milk and warm baths and soft wrappings. I cannot even walk. As for your cattle, wherever they are, they certainly are not here. I swear it by Zeus, the father of us both."

He looked up at Apollo with such a wide and innocent smile that the god could not help laughing, but he was still angry all the same. He picked up the child from the cradle, coverings and all, and shook him. All he got from that was to find out that Hermes was quick and slippery as an eel and could perfectly well stand on his own feet if he chose. At last Apollo, seeing there was nothing to be done with him, took him by the hand and dragged him off to the throne of Zeus upon Olympus. Here the father of gods had to smile as he saw the two of them, the angry god and the curly-haired, blue-eyed child. Hermes stood before his throne and swore in an innocent, baby voice that the cattle had never come near his house, asking indignantly how an infant could be connected with cattle stealing anyway. Zeus laughed, but he knew perfectly well the truth of the affair, and he bade Hermes go immediately and show Apollo where the cattle lay hid. He meant to have no more nonsense, and Hermes saw that he must be obeyed.

Apollo looked down on the hidden meadow to which the child had led him, and saw his great white cattle contentedly feeding there. Then as his eye fell on the hides of the two slaughtered animals stiffening on a rock, he blazed with anger. "You shall pay for this," he said to Hermes, turning on him threateningly.

This time the boy was really frightened and fell back a foot or two, looking uneasily from one side to the other, but he found no escape. "Wait a moment," he begged hastily. "Wait, listen, I have something for you," and he pulled out his lyre. As the god Apollo heard the wonderful notes and perceived how beautifully they would blend with the voice in song, he was amazed and his anger quite fell from him.

"Where did you get this wonderful thing?" he asked. "Give it me, give it me. Keep my fifty cattle, and I will give you a golden staff in addition for you to herd them with. It seems to me I have to have this and to make music for rich feasts and lovely dances. With this I will comfort sorrow, relive past glories, and melt the heart of stone. I think it will sing of itself for me the moment I touch it, for it knows already that it is mine."

"I will gladly give you the lyre," said the son of Maia, "and take your cattle and your golden wand in return. I will be friends with you as a brother ought to be. From now on I swear that I will never steal anything of yours."

Thus the two became friends, and from that time forward Apollo enchanted the gods of Olympus with the glorious music of his lyre. But Hermes drives the white cattle of the sun across the sky on a windy day, and with his golden rod, around which he has twined two snakes, he charms the eyes of men to sleep and deceives them with dreams and visions. Yet Hermes is good for men also, since he rests and heals them with sleep. Moreover he bears the messages of Zeus, and with these he must often do men service.

The Loves of Apollo

Apollo, the young sun god, was more glorious than tongue can describe or than mortal eye can behold. As he drove his golden chariot through the sky he dazzled the whole earth with his splendor. Small wonder, then, that the nymph, Clytie, fell in love with him. Apollo cared nothing for Clytie and would take no notice of her, so that at last her great longing for him drove her almost to madness. She refused to play with her sister nymphs any more, ate nothing, and drank only dew. All night she stood gazing at the heavens, waiting for her lord to appear. All day she followed him with her eyes as he moved slowly from East to West. At last the gods took pity on her, and since she could not die, they changed her into the tall, thin sunflower, which turns its face towards the sun all day as he moves across the sky.

Though Apollo was unkind to Clytie, he too could fall in love. One day in the woods he caught sight of the nymph, Daphne, daughter of a river god. Daphne was fair and white, as river nymphs are, and had rippling dark-green hair. She loved to roam the forests hunting with bow and arrow, and she had vowed to live unmarried like the huntress, Artemis. She, therefore, felt no more love for the god than he had felt for Clytie. Instead she was afraid of him, and when he approached her, she turned and ran from him, her long hair streaming in the wind. More beautiful than ever was she as she ran, and Apollo sped after her, begging her to stop and listen to him, offering her his throne and his palace, telling her not to be afraid. The nearer he came, the more terrified Daphne felt as she raced down the slope towards her father's stream. She felt the radiant warmth of the god behind her, and his hand stretched out to catch her hair. She shrieked to her father to save her, and the river god made answer the only way he could. Suddenly the flight of Daphne was arrested, as her feet took root in the ground. Her body dwindled, her arms shot up, and as Apollo seized her in his arms, he found himself grasping a bush of laurel with shining leaves the color of Daphne's dark-green hair. For a second he felt the frightened heart of the nymph beat beneath the bark enclosing it. Then it was still.

Apollo sorrowed deeply for the loss of his love, and in memory of her he always wore a wreath of laurel. Laurel decorated his lyre, and at his festival the prize for athletes and musicians was a laurel crown.

Phaethon, Son of Apollo

Though Apollo always honored the memory of Daphne, she was not his only love. Another was a mortal, Clymene, by whom he had a son named Phaethon. Phaethon grew up with his mother, who, since she was mortal, could not dwell in the halls of Olympus or in the palace of the sun. She lived not far from the East in the land of Ethiopia, and as her son grew up, she would point to the place where Eos, goddess of the dawn, lighted up the sky and tell him that there his father dwelt. Phaethon loved to boast of his divine father as he saw the golden chariot riding high through the air. He would remind his comrades of other sons of gods and mortal women who, by virtue of their great deeds, had themselves become gods at last. He must always be first in everything, and in most things this was easy, since he was in truth stronger, swifter, and more daring than the others. Even if he were not victorious, Phaethon always claimed to be first in honor. He could never bear to be beaten, even if he must risk his life in some rash way to win.

Most of the princes of Ethiopia willingly paid

Phaethon honor, since they admired him greatly for his fire and beauty. There was one boy, however, Epaphos, who was rumored to be a child of Zeus himself. Since this was not certainly proved, Phaethon chose to disbelieve it and to demand from Epaphos the deference that he obtained from all others. Epaphos was proud too, and one day he lost his temper with Phaethon and turned on him, saying, "You are a fool to believe all that your mother tells you. You are all swelled up with false ideas about your father."

Crimson with rage, the lad rushed home to his mother and demanded that she prove to him the truth of the story that she had often told. "Give me some proof," he implored her, "with which I can answer this insult of Epaphos. It is a matter of life and death to me, for if I cannot, I shall die of shame."

"I swear to you," replied his mother solemnly, "by the bright orb of the sun itself that you are his son. If I swear falsely, may I never look on the sun again, but die before the next time he mounts the heavens. More than this I cannot do, but you, my child, can go to the eastern palace of Phoebus Apollo — it lies not far away — and there speak with the god himself."

The son of Clymene leaped up with joy at his mother's words. The palace of Apollo was indeed not far. It stood just below the eastern horizon, its tall pillars glistening with bronze and gold. Above these it was white with gleaming ivory, and the great doors were flashing silver, embossed with pictures of earth, sky, and sea, and the gods that dwelt therein. Up the steep

hill and the bright steps climbed Phaethon, passing unafraid through the silver doors, and stood in the
presence of the sun. Here at last he was forced to turn
away his face, for Phoebus sat in state on his golden
throne. It gleamed with emeralds and precious stones,
while on the head of the god was a brilliant diamond
crown upon which no eye could look undazzled.

Phaethon hid his face, but the god had recognized
his son, and he spoke kindly, asking him why he had
come. Then Phaethon plucked up courage and said, "I
come to ask you if you are indeed my father. If you are
so, I beg you to give me some proof of it so that all may
recognize me as Phoebus' son."

The god smiled, being well pleased with his son's
beauty and daring. He took off his crown so that
Phaethon could look at him, and coming down from his
throne, he put his arms around the boy, and said, "You
are indeed my son and Clymene's, and worthy to be
called so. Ask of me whatever thing you wish to prove
your origin to men, and you shall have it."

Phaethon swayed for a moment and was dizzy with
excitement at the touch of the god. His heart leaped;
the blood rushed into his face. Now he felt that he was
truly divine, unlike other men, and he did not wish to
be counted with men any more. He looked up for a moment at his radiant father. "Let me drive the chariot of
the sun across the heavens for one day," he said.

Apollo frowned and shook his head. "I cannot break
my promise, but I will dissuade you if I can," he answered. "How can you drive my chariot, whose horses

need a strong hand on the reins? The climb is too steep
for you. The immense height will make you dizzy. The
swift streams of air in the upper heaven will sweep you
off your course. Even the immortal gods could not
drive my chariot. How then can you? Be wise and
make some other choice."

The pride of Phaethon was stubborn, for he thought
the god was merely trying to frighten him. Besides, if he
could guide the sun's chariot, would he not have proved
his right to be divine rather than mortal? For that he
would risk his life. Indeed, once he had seen Apollo's
splendor, he did not wish to go back and live among
men. Therefore, he insisted on his right until Apollo
had to give way.

When the father saw that nothing else would satisfy
the boy, he bade the Hours bring forth his chariot and
yoke the horses. The chariot was of gold and had two
gold-rimmed wheels with spokes of silver. In it there
was room for one man to stand and hold the reins.
Around the front and sides of it ran a rail, but the back
was open. At the end of a long pole there were yokes
for the four horses. The pole was of gold and shone
with precious jewels: the golden topaz, the bright diamond, the green emerald, and the flashing ruby. While
the Hours were yoking the swift, pawing horses, rosy-
fingered Dawn hastened to the gates of heaven to draw
them open. Meanwhile Apollo anointed his son's face
with a magic ointment, that he might be able to bear the
heat of the fire-breathing horses and the golden chariot.
At last Phaethon mounted the chariot and grasped the

reins, the barriers were let down, and the horses shot up into the air.

At first the fiery horses sped forward up the accustomed trail, but behind them the chariot was too light without the weight of the immortal god. It bounded from side to side and was dashed up and down. Phaethon was too frightened and too dizzy to pull the reins, nor would he have known anyway whether he was on the usual path. As soon as the horses felt that there was no hand controlling them, they soared up, up with fiery speed into the heavens till the earth grew pale and cold beneath them. Phaethon shut his eyes, trembling at the dizzy, precipitous height. Then the horses dropped down, more swiftly than a falling stone, flinging themselves madly from side to side in panic because they were masterless. Phaethon dropped the reins entirely and clung with all his might to the chariot rail. Meanwhile as they came near the earth, it dried up and cracked apart. Meadows were reduced to white ashes, cornfields smoked and shriveled, cities perished in flame. Far and wide on the wooded mountains the forests were ablaze, and even the snow-clad Alps were bare and dry. Rivers steamed and dried to dust. The great North African plain was scorched until it became the desert that it is today. Even the sea shrank back to pools and caves, until dried fishes were left baking upon the white-hot sands. At last the great earth mother called upon Zeus to save her from utter destruction, and Zeus hurled a mighty thunderbolt at the unhappy Phaethon, who was still crouched in the chariot, clinging desperately to the rail. The dart cast him out, and he fell flaming in a long trail through the air. The chariot broke in pieces at the mighty blow, and the maddened horses rushed snorting back to the stable of their master, Apollo.

Unhappy Clymene and her daughters wandered over the whole earth seeking the body of the boy they loved so well. When they found him, they took him and buried him. Over his grave they wept and could not be comforted. At last the gods in pity for their grief changed them into poplar trees, which weep with tears of amber in memory of Phaethon.

Athene's City

In the days when Greece was first being settled, Cecrops was king in Attica, a rugged, triangular little country, good mainly for goat farming and the culture of honey bees, and surrounded on two sides by the sea. Here Cecrops planned a city around a steep rock that jutted from the plain a few miles inland. Down on the shore were two fine harbors, while around spread fertile country watered by two streams. The gods, who were always interested in the affairs of men, approved the idea of Cecrops and gave the new city their blessing, foreseeing that it would become in time one of the famous cities of the world. For this reason there was great dispute among the gods as to which of them should be its special patron. Many claims were put forward by this god or by that, but at last, after much arguing, it became clear that the award should lie between Athene, goddess of wisdom, and the sea god, Poseidon. Between these two the gods decided to have a contest. Each should produce some marvel in the Attic land, and each should promise some gift to the city that was to come. The greater gift should win the city.

When the appointed day came, the judges ranged themselves on the rock, and the two gods came before them. Some say that the twelve judges chosen were the spirits of the Attic hills and rivers, and some maintain that they were twelve Olympian gods. Be that as it may, on one side stood Poseidon with flowing dark-blue beard and majestic stature, carrying in his hand the three-pronged trident with which he rules the waves. On the other side stood Athene, grey-eyed and serene, helmet on her golden head and spear in hand. At the word Poseidon raised his trident and struck the ground. Beneath the feet of the judges the whole earth was terribly shaken, and with a mighty rumbling sound it split apart before them. Then appeared the marvel, a salt spring four miles inland where no water had appeared before. To this Poseidon added his gift of sea power, promising the city a great empire, a mighty navy, famed shipwrights, and trading vessels which should make her name known in every corner of the sea.

The judges looked at one another as Poseidon spoke and nodded their heads in approval, thinking the gift indeed a great one and the salt spring and the earthquake fine symbols of Poseidon's power. Grey-eyed Athene said nothing, but smiled gently to herself as she laid aside her spear and quietly kneeling down appeared to plant something in the earth. Between her hands as she worked, there gradually unfolded a little tree, a bush rather, small and unimpressive, with grey-green leaves and grey-green berries about an inch in length. When it had grown to full size, Athene stood up and looked at the judges. That was all.

Poseidon glanced at the dusty looking bush that had grown so quietly. He looked at the hole that had gaped in the earth with the thunder of earthquake, and he threw back his head and laughed. Round the bay rumbled and re-echoed the laughter of the god like distant waves thundering on the rocks, while far out to sea in their deep, green caverns, the old sea gods, his subjects, sent a muffled answering roar. Presently as silence fell, the quiet voice of Athene spoke to the assembled gods.

"This little shrub is the olive, at the same time my marvel and my gift to the city," she said. "With these berries the poor man will flavor his coarse bread and goat's-milk cheese. With scented oil the rich man will deck himself for the feast. Oil poured to the gods shall be among their favorite offerings. With it the housewife will light her lamp and do her cooking, and the athlete will cleanse himself from dust and sweat. This is the ware merchants will carry in the ships Poseidon speaks of, to gain riches and renown for the city which sells what all men use. Moreover, I will make its people skilled in pottery, so that the jars in which the oil is carried shall themselves be a marvel, and the city shall flourish and be famous, not only in trade but in the arts."

She finished, and the judges cried out in surprise at the richness of her dull-looking gift. They awarded the prize to Athene, who called the city Athens. Long afterwards when Athens became famous, celebrated for its beauty and wisdom, the Athenians built a great temple in honor of their patron goddess. This temple was called the Parthenon, or temple of the maiden goddess. Though in ruins, it is still standing and is one of the most famous buildings of the world. Round it are two rows of columns and above these a sloping roof. At one end in the triangular space between the slope of the roof and the tops of the columns, a famous sculptor carved a representation of Athene's contest. These statues are nearly all destroyed, and the great gold and ivory image of Athene has disappeared from within the building; but we still have the frieze that went right around the temple, on which is carved a picture of the annual procession of the Athenians in honor of their goddess. There are the young men mounting their horses, or slowly moving off as the procession starts. There are horsemen and chariots already in column. On foot go lyre-players, making music and singing in honor of the goddess. Men drive cattle for sacrifice, and the fairest maidens of the city are carrying baskets of flowers. A new and beautiful robe is being brought to offer to the image of the goddess of weaving. Apart, the Olympian gods upon their thrones behold the scene, while within the temple priests and priestesses make ready to receive the offerings for the goddess. These things can still be seen, but the original olive tree has long vanished, while even the mark of Poseidon's trident, which used to be shown for centuries, has disappeared.

Arachne

A rachne was a maiden who became famous throughout Greece, though she was neither well-born nor beautiful and came from no great city. She lived in an obscure little village, and her father was a humble dyer of wool. In this he was very skillful, producing many varied shades, while above all he was famous for the clear, bright scarlet which is made from shellfish, and which was the most glorious of all the colors used in ancient Greece. Even more skillful than her father was Arachne. It was her task to spin the fleecy wool into a fine, soft thread and to weave it into cloth on the high, standing loom within the cottage. Arachne was small and pale from much working. Her eyes were light and her hair was a dusty brown, yet she was quick and graceful, and her fingers, roughened as they were, went so fast that it was hard to follow their flickering movements. So soft and even was her thread, so fine her cloth, so gorgeous her embroidery, that soon her products were known all over Greece. No one had ever seen the like of them before.

At last Arachne's fame became so great that people

used to come from far and wide to watch her working. Even the graceful nymphs would steal in from stream or forest and peep shyly through the dark doorway, watching in wonder the white arms of Arachne as she stood at the loom and threw the shuttle from hand to hand between the hanging threads, or drew out the long wool, fine as a hair, from the distaff as she sat spinning. "Surely Athene herself must have taught her," people would murmur to one another. "Who else could know the secret of such marvelous skill?"

Arachne was used to being wondered at, and she was immensely proud of the skill that had brought so many to look on her. Praise was all she lived for, and it displeased her greatly that people should think anyone, even a goddess, could teach her anything. Therefore when she heard them murmur, she would stop her work and turn round indignantly to say, "With my own ten fingers I gained this skill, and by hard practice from early morning till night. I never had time to stand looking as you people do while another maiden worked. Nor if I had, would I give Athene credit because the girl was more skillful than I. As for Athene's weaving, how could there be finer cloth or more beautiful embroidery than mine? If Athene herself were to come down and compete with me, she could do no better than I."

One day when Arachne turned round with such words, an old woman answered her, a grey old woman, bent and very poor, who stood leaning on a staff and peering at Arachne amid the crowd of onlookers.

"Reckless girl," she said, "how dare you claim to be equal to the immortal gods themselves? I am an old woman and have seen much. Take my advice and ask pardon of Athene for your words. Rest content with your fame of being the best spinner and weaver that mortal eyes have ever beheld."

"Stupid old woman," said Arachne indignantly, "who gave you a right to speak in this way to me? It is easy to see that you were never good for anything in your day, or you would not come here in poverty and rags to gaze at my skill. If Athene resents my words, let her answer them herself. I have challenged her to a contest, but she, of course, will not come. It is easy for the gods to avoid matching their skill with that of men."

At these words the old woman threw down her staff and stood erect. The wondering onlookers saw her grow tall and fair and stand clad in long robes of dazzling white. They were terribly afraid as they realized that they stood in the presence of Athene. Arachne herself flushed red for a moment, for she had never really believed that the goddess would hear her. Before the group that was gathered there she would not give in; so pressing her pale lips together in obstinacy and pride, she led the goddess to one of the great looms and set herself before the other. Without a word both began to thread the long woolen strands that hang from the rollers, and between which the shuttle moves back and forth. Many skeins lay heaped beside them to use, bleached white, and gold, and scarlet, and other shades, varied as the rainbow. Arachne had never thought of giving credit for her success to her father's skill in dyeing, though in actual truth the colors were as remarkable as the cloth itself.

Soon there was no sound in the room but the breathing of the onlookers, the whirring of the shuttles, and the creaking of the wooden frames as each pressed the thread up into place or tightened the pegs by which the whole was held straight. The excited crowd in the doorway began to see that the skill of both in truth was very nearly equal, but that, however the cloth might turn out, the goddess was the quicker of the two. A pattern of many pictures was growing on her loom. There was a border of twined branches of the olive, Athene's favorite tree, while in the middle, figures began to appear. As they looked at the glowing colors, the spectators realized that Athene was weaving into her pattern a last warning to Arachne. The central figure was the goddess herself competing with Poseidon for possession of the city of Athens; but in the four corners were mortals who had tried to strive with gods and pictures of the awful fate that had overtaken them. The goddess ended a little before Arachne and stood back from her marvelous work to see what the maiden was doing.

Never before had Arachne been matched against anyone whose skill was equal, or even nearly equal to her own. As she stole glances from time to time at Athene and saw the goddess working swiftly, calmly, and always a little faster than herself, she became angry instead of frightened, and an evil thought came into her head. Thus as Athene stepped back a pace to watch Arachne finishing her work, she saw that the maiden had taken for her design a pattern of scenes which showed evil or unworthy actions of the gods, how they had deceived fair maidens, resorted to trickery, and appeared on earth from time to time in the form of poor and humble people. When the goddess saw this insult glowing in bright colors on Arachne's loom, she did not wait while the cloth was judged, but stepped forward, her grey eyes blazing with anger, and tore Arachne's work across. Then she struck Arachne across the face. Arachne stood there a moment, struggling with anger, fear, and pride. "I will not live under this insult," she cried, and seizing a rope from the wall, she made a noose and would have hanged herself.

The goddess touched the rope and touched the maiden. "Live on, wicked girl," she said. "Live on and spin, both you and your descendants. When men look at you they may remember that it is not wise to strive with Athene." At that the body of Arachne shrivelled up, and her legs grew tiny, spindly, and distorted. There before the eyes of the spectators hung a little dusty brown spider on a slender thread.

All spiders descend from Arachne, and as the Greeks watched them spinning their thread wonderfully fine, they remembered the contest with Athene and thought that it was not right for even the best of men to claim equality with the gods.

The Origin of the Seasons

Demeter, the great earth mother, was goddess of the harvest. Tall and majestic was her appearance, and her hair was the color of ripe wheat. It was she who filled the ears with grain. In her honor white-robed women brought golden garlands of wheat as first fruits to the altar. Reaping, threshing, winnowing, and the long tables set in the shade for the harvesters' refreshment—all these were hers. Songs and feasting did her honor as the hard-working farmer gathered his abundant fruit. All the laws which the farmer knew came from her: the time for plowing, what land would best bear crops, which was fit for grapes, and which to leave for pasture. She was a goddess whom men called the great mother because of her generosity in giving. Her own special daughter in the family of the gods was named Persephone.

Persephone was the spring maiden, young and full of joy. Sicily was her home, for it is a land where the spring is long and lovely, and where spring flowers are abundant. Here Persephone played with her maidens from day to day till the rocks and valleys rang with the sound of laughter, and gloomy Hades heard it as he sat on his throne in the dark land of the dead. Even his heart of stone was touched by her gay young beauty, so that he arose in his awful majesty and came up to Olympus to ask Zeus if he might have Persephone to wife. Zeus bowed his head in agreement, and mighty Olympus thundered as he promised.

Thus it came about that as Persephone was gathering flowers with her maidens in the vale of Enna, a marvelous thing happened. Enna was a beautiful valley in whose meadows all the most lovely flowers of the year grew at the same season. There were wild roses, purple crocuses, sweet-scented violets, tall iris, rich narcissus, and white lilies. All these the girl was gathering, yet fair as they were, Persephone herself was fairer far.

As the maidens went picking and calling to one another across the blossoming meadow, it happened that Persephone strayed apart from the rest. Then as she looked a little ahead in the meadow, she suddenly beheld the marvelous thing. It was a flower so beautiful that none like it had ever been known. It seemed a kind of narcissus, purple and white, but from a single root there sprang a hundred blossoms, and at the sweet scent of it the very heavens and earth appeared to smile for joy. Without calling to the others, Persephone sprang forward to be the first to pick the precious bloom. As she stretched out her hand, the earth opened in front of her, and she found herself caught in a stranger's arms. Persephone shrieked aloud and struggled, while the armful of flowers cascaded down to earth. However, the dark-eyed Hades was far stronger than she. He swept her into his golden chariot, took the reins of his coal-black horses, and was gone amid the rumbling sound of the closing earth before the other girls in the valley could even come in sight of the spot. When they did get there, nobody was visible. Only the roses and lilies of Persephone lay scattered in wild confusion over the grassy turf.

Bitter was the grief of Demeter when she heard the news of her daughter's mysterious fate. Veiling herself with a dark cloud she sped, swift as a wild bird, over land and ocean for nine days, searching everywhere and asking all she met if they had seen her daughter. Neither gods nor men had seen her. Even the birds could give no tidings, and Demeter in despair turned to Phoebus Apollo, who sees all things from his chariot in the heavens.

"Yes, I have seen your daughter," said the god at last. "Hades has taken her with the consent of Zeus, that she may dwell in the land of mist and gloom as his queen. The girl struggled and was unwilling, but Hades is far stronger than she."

When she heard this, Demeter fell into deep despair, for she knew she could never rescue Persephone if Zeus and Hades had agreed. She did not care any more to enter the palace of Olympus where the gods live in joy and feasting and where Apollo plays the lyre while the Muses sing. She took on her the form of an old woman, worn but stately, and wandered about the earth, where there is much sorrow to be seen. At first she kept away from the homes of people, since the sight of little children and happy mothers gave her pain. One day, however, as she sat by the side of a well to rest her weary feet, four girls came down to draw water. They were kind-hearted and charming as they talked with her and concerned themselves about the fate of the homeless stranger woman who was sitting at their gates. To account for herself, Demeter told them that she was a woman of good family from Crete across the sea who had been captured by pirates and was to have been sold for a slave. She had escaped as they landed once to cook a meal on shore, and now she was wandering to find work.

The four girls listened to this story, much impressed by the stately manner of the strange woman. At last they said that their mother, Metaneira, was looking for a nurse for their new-born brother, Demophoon. Perhaps the stranger would come and talk with her. Demeter agreed, feeling a great longing to hold a baby once more, even if it were not her own. She went therefore to Metaneira, who was much struck with the quiet dignity of the goddess and glad to give her charge of her little son. For a while thereafter Demeter was nurse to Demophoon, and his smiles and babble consoled her in some part for her own darling daughter. She began to make plans for Demophoon: he should be a great hero; he should become an immortal, so that when he grew up she could keep him with her.

Presently the whole household was amazed at how beautiful Demophoon was growing, the more so as they never saw the nurse feed him anything. Secretly Demeter would anoint him with ambrosia, like the gods, and from her breath as he lay in her lap, he would draw his nourishment. When the night came, she would linger by the great fireside in the hall, rocking the child in her arms while the embers burned low and the people went off to sleep. Then when all was still, she would stoop quickly down and put the baby into the fire itself. All night long the child would sleep in the red-hot ashes, while his earthly flesh and blood changed slowly into the substance of the immortals. In the morning when people came, the ashes were cold and dead, and by the hearth sat the stranger-woman, gently rocking and singing to the child.

Presently Metaneira became suspicious of the strangeness of it all. What did she know of this nurse but the story she had heard from her daughters? Perhaps the woman was a witch of some sort who wished to steal or transform the boy. In any case it was wise to be careful. One night, therefore, when she went up to her chamber, she set the door ajar and stood there in the crack silently watching the nurse at the fireside crooning over the child. The hall was very dark, so that it was hard to see clearly, but in a little while the mother beheld the dim figure bend forward. A log broke in the fireplace, a little flame shot up, and there clear in the light lay the baby on top of the fire.

Metaneira screamed loudly and lost no time in rushing forward, but it was Demeter who snatched up the

baby. "Fool that you are," she said indignantly to Metaneira, "I would have made your son immortal, but that
is now impossible. He shall be a great hero, but in the
end he will have to die. I, the goddess Demeter, promise
it." With that old age fell from her and she grew in
stature. Golden hair spread down over her shoulders so
that the great hall was filled with light. She turned and
went out of the doorway, leaving the baby on the
ground and Metaneira too amazed and frightened even
to take him up.

All the while that Demeter had been wandering, she
had given no thought to her duties as the harvest goddess. Instead she was almost glad that others should
suffer because she was suffering. In vain the oxen spent
their strength in dragging the heavy plowshare through
the soil. In vain did the sower with his bag of grain
throw out the even handfuls of white barley in a wide
arc as he strode. The greedy birds had a feast off the
seed corn that season, or if it started to sprout, sun
baked it and rains washed it away. Nothing would
grow. As the gods looked down, they saw threatening
the earth a famine such as never had been known. Even
the offerings to the gods were neglected by despairing
men who could no longer spare anything from their
dwindling stores.

At last Zeus sent Iris, the rainbow, to seek out
Demeter and appeal to her to save mankind. Dazzling
Iris swept down from Olympus swift as a ray of light
and found Demeter sitting in her temple, the dark cloak

still around her and her head bowed on her hand. Though Iris urged her with the messages of Zeus and offered beautiful gifts or whatever powers among the gods she chose, Demeter would not lift her head or listen. All she said was that she would neither set foot on Olympus nor let fruit grow on the earth until Persephone was restored to her from the kingdom of the dead.

At last Zeus saw that he must send Hermes of the golden sandals to bring back Persephone to the light. The messenger found dark-haired Hades sitting upon his throne with Persephone beside him, pale and sad. She had neither eaten nor drunk since she had been in the land of the dead. She sprang up with joy at the message of Hermes, while the dark king looked gloomier than ever, for he really loved his queen. Though he could not disobey the command of Zeus, he was crafty, and he pressed Persephone to eat or drink with him as they parted. Now, with joy in her heart, she should not refuse all food. Persephone was eager to be gone, but since the king entreated her, she took a pomegranate from him to avoid argument and delay. Giving in to his pleading, she ate seven of the seeds. Then Hermes took her with him, and she came out into the upper air.

When Demeter saw Hermes with her daughter, she started up, and Persephone too rushed forward with a glad cry and flung her arms about her mother's neck. For a long time the two caressed each other, but at last Demeter began to question the girl. "Did you eat or drink anything with Hades?" she asked her daughter anxiously, and the girl replied:

"Nothing until Hermes released me. Then in my joy I took a pomegranate and ate seven of its seeds."

"Alas," said the goddess in dismay, "my daughter, what have you done? The Fates have said that if you ate anything in the land of shadow, you must return to Hades and rule with him as his queen. However, you ate not the whole pomegranate, but only seven of the seeds. For seven months of the year, therefore, you must dwell in the underworld, and the remaining five you may live with me."

Thus the Fates had decreed, and even Zeus could not alter their law. For seven months of every year Persephone is lost to Demeter and rules pale and sad over the dead. At this time Demeter mourns, trees shed their leaves, cold comes, and the earth lies still and dead. But when in the eighth month Persephone returns, her mother is glad and the earth rejoices. The wheat springs up, bright, fresh, and green in the plowland. Flowers unfold, birds sing, and young animals are born. Everywhere the heavens smile for joy or weep sudden showers of gladness upon the springing earth.

The Mysteries of Dionysus

Dionysus, or Bacchus, god of wine, was one of the gods most important to daily life in Greece. Wine mixed with water was the common drink of both rich and poor. The cultivation of the vine was the common care of every farmer, so that the harvesting and the treading of the grapes in the wine press were almost as important events as the reaping which was sacred to Demeter. Then too Dionysus was a particularly human god. Wine made the tongue loosen and the heart be at ease. It was associated with gaiety and feasting. It brought refreshment after a day of toil, and sound sleep to the weary or sorrowful. For all these reasons the Greeks thought of Dionysus as a god who was in his way very close to them. He dwelt on earth more than on Olympus. He was born late, in the age of mortal heroes rather than the age of gods, and he was born of a mortal woman. Semele, a princess of the royal house of Thebes, was his mother. Zeus loved her, and she implored him to appear to her in his divine glory, but when she had persuaded him to do so, she was burned to ashes by the fire of his heavenly presence. Zeus saved the infant and sent him to Asia to be brought up. There he lived in the woodland glades with the nymphs and satyrs, who were little, goat-legged gods with pointed ears and shaggy hair, followers of Pan, the great god of the woodlands. These played with Dionysus, while old, fat Silenus was tutor to the child. At least it was so at first, but as the boy grew older, it was he who led and the others who followed him.

Dionysus became a beautiful young god with long, curling locks and the pink-and-white complexion of one who feasts in shady halls rather than running, wrestling, or working in the open air. Yet he was in a way an outdoor god, and those who followed him were woodland creatures. When he was grown and the time was come, he gave to man the vine and traveled with it through all the eastern lands across to India. He returned thence across Asia and came finally to Greece. With him came all the nymphs and satyrs, laughing and dancing about the car in which he rode, while behind him followed old Silenus, rolling from side to side on the back of an ass. He himself stood in his car wreathed with ivy, and all the noisy crowd about him had ivy and vine leaves in their hair. They stripped rods from the trees, twining them with ivy and vine, and since men love music with feasting, they had pipes to entertain them and the rhythmic beat of clashing cymbals to which they danced. All sorts of wild beasts joined Dionysus' train, their savagery forgotten under the influence of wine. Leopards drew his ivy car. Spotted lynxes and lions followed him. The whole group, dancing, reveling, and making wild music, poured through the land, leaving the vine wherever they went and instituting the rites of Dionysus.

The ceremonies of Dionysus were mysteries. That is to say, they were secret from all but those who had been initiated. They were held outside the cities on the mountains or in the woodland and were open to anyone, though they concerned chiefly women. The women worshipers were called Bacchantes after the other name of Dionysus, and they were smitten by the god with a mad frenzy. When, for instance, he came to Thebes, his mother's home, the people would not receive him, and in revenge he maddened the women. They left their homes, their husbands, and their young children, and poured out of the city one and all, from fair-haired girl to toothless grandmother, to revel with Dionysus on the mountains. There, clothed in skins of leopard or of fawn, they wreathed their streaming hair with ivy, split wands from trees, and ran laughing and shrieking through the woods. Nothing could hurt them in their ecstasy. In sudden frenzy they would hunt savage beasts and tear them limb from limb. Even Pentheus, king of Thebes and Dionysus' greatest enemy, was slain in this way as he went out to spy on the mysterious revels. His own mother and her followers fell on him and, taking him for a mountain lion in their madness, killed him.

Such were the Bacchic revels, for if Dionysus was often kindly, he could be fierce and terrible. One story says that as he stood alone on a headland that overlooked the sea, some pirates saw him and, noting his rich garments of scarlet and gold, determined to capture him. They made for shore, seized him, and thrust him into their ship. Then the rest of them took up the oars and put their backs into the work, lest in a moment the alarm be sounded and the friends of this rich young prince come out to rescue him. The helmsman, however, kept watch on the prisoner and saw a smile in his dark eyes, while the bonds fell off his hands and feet as though they had never been tied. At that he guessed the truth and called out in terror to his companions, "This is no prince that we have in our boat, but a god. Bonds cannot hold him. Let us set him on shore at once, lest he loose a tempest on us and destroy us."

The captain, however, had no glance to spare for the prisoner. His mind was already dwelling on the rich ransom he would get. Without taking any notice of the helmsman, he ordered his men to hoist the sail. Even as they seized the sheets, a strange scent of wine filled the air, and the rowers bending forward saw a dark trickle flowing past their feet. Then a vine spread suddenly along the top of the square sail. It put out flowers while they gaped at it. Tendrils wriggled down the mast, and dark purple clusters hung down across the canvas. Up the mast from the deck coiled an ivy stalk to meet the vine. Berries and blossoms grew out upon it as it mounted. Even the oars grew garlands until the rowers could move no more. They called out in panic to the helmsman to see if he could put them in to land, but it was too late to get rid of their dangerous passenger.

Amidships a black, shaggy bear stood up from nowhere with a growl and lurched towards them. As they recoiled, from behind them came a far louder roar, and there in the bows beside the god, a lion crouched ready to spring. Before anyone had time to make a movement, the lion had the captain in his jaws. At that the pirates jumped overboard with screams of fright and were changed there into black dolphins. Only the helmsman was left on the deserted ship, for Dionysus saved him because he had urged the others to release the god. As he guided the helm, the ship of itself sailed the god across to Greece.

Dionysus is also important because he was god of tragedy. Every year at his festival there was a dramatic contest in the outdoor theatre at Athens. Three playwrights were chosen, each of whom wrote three tragedies, presenting some one of the legends of ancient Greece. All the citizens of Athens went to listen, and a prize was given to the man whose plays were judged the best. Plays were written in honor of Dionysus by some of the greatest dramatists of all time. These have made the name and festival of Dionysus famous even today.

II

THE LOVES OF
THE GODS

Cupid and Psyche

A certain king in Greece had three daughters. The eldest two, who were good-looking girls, were well and richly married, but the youngest, whose name was Psyche, was more beautiful than men had ever dreamed of. Hundreds came daily to her father's palace simply to behold her, while far and wide the rumor ran that she was the golden-haired goddess Aphrodite herself, the queen of beauty appearing to mankind on earth. Indeed, so dazzling was Psyche's beauty that men came not to woo her but to worship her. No one asked for her hand in marriage, but the palace steps and courtyards were piled high with offerings of fruit, flowers, cattle, gold ornaments, and precious embroidery. Meanwhile, the temples of Aphrodite, once thronged, were dead and empty, since men preferred to pray and sacrifice to the living Psyche rather than to the marble images in the temples of the goddess.

Now Aphrodite, goddess of beauty, was the most temperamental of all the gods. Thus when she saw that her worship was neglected, she was furiously jealous of the innocent Psyche and begged her son to take a terrible revenge. Eros, whom we know better as Cupid, was a tall young man with fair, smooth cheeks and golden hair, rosy-winged, and armed with a golden bow. He was the god of love, and his arrows were arrows of desire. Aphrodite bade him take his bow, choose out some loathsome monster, and strike the heart of Psyche that she might fall in love with it and bring herself into dreadful misfortune.

Meantime, the king, Psyche's father, was frightened by the notice that his daughter was getting. He well knew how easy it was to arouse the jealousy of the immortals, and he would gladly have married off his daughter to some prince of a distant land. There he hoped the people would regard her as a queen, not as a goddess. Since, however, no man had dared to ask for Psyche as a wife, he was hard put to it to find a way out of the difficulty. At last he decided to send a message to the oracle to ask Apollo who it was that Psyche should have for a husband, but when he received the answer of the oracle, he was bitterly sorry that he had asked. The riddling rhyme of the oracle hinted at a strange beast, a winged monster — maybe a dragon or a serpent, the wise men thought. Furthermore, it demanded that Psyche be led immediately outside the city up to the top of a great, towering rock, and there left to meet her fate. Fond as he was of his daughter, the king dared not disobey the oracle's direct command. It was the custom in those days to take the bride to her husband's house with a great procession. Therefore the king made all ready as though for a bride, but the pinewood torches were black and smoking, the pipes played a dirge, not a wedding dance, and instead of acrobats and dancers, mourners, clad in black, led the procession. With weeping and lamentation they brought Psyche to the rock and left her to endure what might befall.

Psyche was caught up by a gentle wind and carried away to a very pleasant valley where she was set gently down in a flowering meadow. Before her was a shady grove and a bubbling stream, while by the stream she saw a marvelous house. It was built of ivory inlaid with silver, and the pillars were of gold. When she came nearer, she saw the entrance was paved with glowing pictures made out of various bright stones. As she went wondering through the open doors and caught a glimpse of the treasures within, a soft voice spoke to her out of the air, saying, "Fair Psyche, all this wealth is at your command. We whose voices you hear are your servants. We will prepare for you a bath, lay out fresh garments, and serve you with whatever food you wish."

This they did, and as Psyche ate, the invisible spirits played soft music and sang to her, while all around she heard sounds as though she were sitting at a banquet with a multitude of people.

At night, Psyche took one of the little oil lamps whose unprotected flame burned clear and steady in the stillness of the air and went to bed. Then when all was dark someone came to her room who kissed her, and made love to her, and called himself her husband.

They talked together in the darkness until they fell
asleep, but when Psyche awoke in the morning, her
husband was gone without her having seen his face.

Things went on in this way for some while. All day
long Psyche lived by herself in the ivory palace sur-
rounded by invisible servants who hastened to fulfill
every desire. Every night when the lamp was out, her
husband came to her room and stayed with her. Before
light came, he vanished, and always he impressed upon
her that she must not try to find out who he was lest terrible misfortune follow. Psyche was content at first, for
she loved her husband, but during the long hours of the
day when she was alone, she thought often of her parents and her sisters and of the great distress they must
be feeling upon her account. Finally she could bear it
no longer and asked her husband for news of them.

"Your sisters have gone up to the rock from which I
took you," he replied, "and there they are mourning as
though you were dead."

When Psyche heard this, she implored her husband
to let her sisters visit her that she might show them she
was well and happy and give them messages for her
parents. He was very unwilling to grant this at first, for
he feared that the sisters would question Psyche too
closely as to what sort of person he was. However,
Psyche begged him, saying that she was very unhappy;
so at last he gave in.

The next morning when her sisters came to the rock
and searched all around it weeping and calling, Psyche
heard and answered them, commanding the wind to lift

them up and set them down in the valley where she now was. Then she came out and fell on their necks with great rejoicing. After a while, when she had kissed and comforted them, she led them into her house. She showed them all the beauty of it with its treasures of gold and silver, her rich garments, and her invisible servants who offered them refreshment and played and sang to them while they ate. As for her husband, she pretended he was away for a while, inventing quickly something to satisfy her sisters. But when she saw that they were becoming too curious, she said their visit must end this time and, loading them with gifts and many messages, she sent them back as they had come.

The sisters went on their way with gold and precious jewels, but as they came down from the rock where the wind had left them, they began to talk with envy of Psyche's luck.

"It is not fair," said the eldest, "that our youngest sister, who set herself up to be a goddess and caused our parents all this sorrow, should now be so fortunate."

"No indeed," answered the other. "We two have worshiped the gods and done our duty. Yet we have been married off into distant countries, you to a man almost as old as our father, and I to one who has the gout and is always ailing. Psyche was always the favorite. Now if we tell what we have seen, she will be more beloved than ever. Let us hide the gifts she gave us and pretend we could not find her. What cares she for us and her parents?"

Accordingly the two wicked sisters hid Psyche's presents and said nothing of having seen her, leaving their parents to mourn their lost daughter and to make much of the two that were left.

In the meantime Psyche, suspecting nothing, had only pleasant memories of her sisters. For some time she was happy, but presently she grew lonely again and asked her husband if she might see them once more. He gave consent to this unwillingly, for he was suspicious of them, but since Psyche's heart was set on it, he could not deny her. This time the sisters were full of flattery, and the visit went off well until they began to question her curiously about her husband. At this Psyche became confused, trying to put them off with vague answers, for she had forgotten exactly what she had said before. The two persisted when they saw her at a loss and began to notice that her account of her husband did not agree at all with her former one. As they went home that day they put their heads together and hit on the truth, namely that Psyche had never seen her husband and actually did not know what he was like. Here they saw their opportunity to make trouble, and when they visited Psyche for the third time, they forced her to admit that this was indeed the case.

"Alas, my poor Psyche," said the elder sister, "can it really be that you do not know your dreadful fate and why your husband has forbidden you to see him? He is a great serpent whom hunters have often watched swim across the river to this place. Did not the oracle of Apollo warn you that you would marry a fearful monster? To be sure, he is kind to you now, but presently he will grow tired. One night when he comes to your chamber, he will seize upon you, and you will die horribly in his jaws." With that she and her sister wept so convincingly that Psyche was almost terrified out of her wits.

"What shall I do," she stammered fearfully, "to save myself from this?"

"Take a knife with you to bed," said the elder sister, "and hide it till your husband is asleep. Then get up quietly and fetch the lamp that you always carry to your bedroom. By the light of this you will see the monster and may cut off his head."

In fear and trembling Psyche promised to follow her sisters' advice, so that now these two departed happily, sure that they had caused trouble. Either Psyche's husband was indeed a monster, or if he were not, at least he would be angry with her for having disobeyed him.

In the middle of the night Psyche rose very gently, feeling for her knife, and stole barefoot across the room to fetch the lamp. At every movement from the bed she held her breath, but soon the flickering little flame was alight. Slowly, foot by foot she crept back, holding the lamp high and peering at the form that lay turned away from her on the bed. Finally she stood right over him and saw all clearly. It was Cupid, the god of love himself. It was he, and she could not be mistaken. He lay there, long dark lashes closed and golden curls all rumpled, one hand beneath his cheek. On his shoulders rested white wings, each feather tipped with rose, while at the foot of the bed his golden bow and arrows glit-

tered strangely as the lamp wavered in her trembling
hand. Psyche gave a great start of fear and joy, and
with that a drop of burning oil fell from her lamp onto
the right shoulder of the god. At this he started up with
a cry and seeing Psyche, with the lamp still raised in her
left hand and the forgotten knife in her right, he cried,
"Oh faithless wife, would you spy out my secret against
my express command? I will take vengeance on your
sisters for this, and as for you, since you cannot be true
to me, I will come no more." With that he spread his
wings and fled away.

The unfortunate Psyche dropped the knife and the
lamp by the bedside where she stood, and ran through
the house and down to the river after her husband, calling out to him as she went. When he sped on over the
river without even once looking back, she threw herself
in, desperate to follow him or die. She might have
drowned but that the river pitied her and carrying her
far downstream, cast her up gently on a grassy bank.
From there she wandered far and wide seeking Cupid,
till at last in desperation she came into Aphrodite's temple, thinking that from Cupid's mother, even though her
enemy, she might gain news.

For a long time after Aphrodite had told her son to
punish Psyche, she suspected nothing, but finally the
white sea gull, which is Aphrodite's favorite bird, sped
to her with news of what had been going on. Aphrodite
was filled with fury against Psyche and her son. She
had already forbidden Cupid to see his wife again. Now
she determined to take revenge. She therefore had the

girl brought before her and spoke mockingly to her, abusing her for having dared as a mortal to marry with a god. Since she had laid claim to godhead in this fashion, let her show that she could do as gods do. With that Aphrodite had her servants bring in sacks of different grain, barley, poppy seed, beans, peas, lentils, and many others. These she poured out on the stone floor of the temple, all mingled together. Then she bade Psyche sort them out. "Since you are a goddess, you can finish it by nightfall," said she. With that she swept away, threatening fearful torments if the task were not performed, while poor Psyche sat on the cold floor, gazing with despair on the mountainous heap.

Though Cupid was angry with Psyche, he had not forgotten her. He dared not openly disobey his mother, but presently Psyche found herself idly watching a small black ant who was dragging away a grain of poppy seed. Then she saw another with a grain of barley, and presently two more struggling with a pea. In a few minutes the whole heap was alive with ants who were picking up the grains and carrying them one by one to separate heaps. Almost it seemed as though the grains were moving of themselves. By the last rays of the sun she saw the whole was sorted, and she wept tears of joy because she had escaped the anger of the goddess and because she saw that Cupid had protected her. The last rays shone too on the white feet of the golden goddess, who had come to see what had happened. At the sight she was angry indeed, for she knew it was the work of Cupid. Nevertheless she had no excuse to punish Psyche and merely threatened her with another task on the next day.

Next morning Aphrodite bade Psyche look across the river at some great, shining sheep that were grazing on a green meadow. The goddess demanded some of their golden wool, but Psyche went down to the river side to throw herself in and end her sorrows rather than to find a crossing place. As she came near, the wind in the reeds made murmuring music, and when she bent over the edge, she could hear what it was saying.

"Psyche, beware of the terrible sheep, for they are savage as the wild boar in the woods. Wait till the midday sun shines down on their golden fleece and makes them hot and heavy. Then they will come galloping down to the river bank, tearing through the brambles and thickets in their eagerness to drink. But when they have drunk and refreshed themselves, they will go back to their meadow. Then you may cross the river and gather from the brambles the wool that they have left there. Thus you may save your life and satisfy the goddess."

When she heard this, Psyche grew glad again, since she knew that Cupid was caring for her. She did exactly as the wind said and came home at evening to Aphrodite with an armful of the wool. When the goddess saw Psyche thus again successful, she flew into a passion and determined once and for all to get rid of the girl. This time she handed her a bottle and said, "Fill this bottle for me with the water of the Styx. There it lies."

Pointing out a dreadful dark chasm in a mountain side, she left Psyche once more to her fate.

The Styx was a black and deadly river that flowed through the underworld as a boundary to the home of the dead. So terrible were its waters that even the spirits could not cross through its stream but had to pay Charon, the ghostly ferryman, to carry them over. But Charon would not carry the unburied dead. These wandered up and down the grey mud of the river banks, always seeking to cross, but never daring to enter the waters, and the high, thin sound of their wailing echoed across the stream.

When Psyche entered the black gorge where the dreadful river flowed down into the earth, the great reptiles who live on the mud banks raised their scaly snouts and opened their dull eyes to blink at her. She was terribly afraid and stood as though turned to stone, unable, like the dead, to approach the stream. Straightway an eagle, the royal messenger of Zeus, snatched the bottle from her hand, flew far out over the monsters, and filled it with the water. Once more Psyche went successful into the presence of Aphrodite.

This time Aphrodite was astonished, but she merely held out to Psyche a little box, saying, "Take this box down to Hades and ask the queen of the underworld to fill it with a little of her beauty. If the Styx does not frighten you, surely you can cross into the land of the dead."

Men had gone down into the land of Hades and re-

turned again, but only a very few, and these were heroes of mighty strength or under the protection of the gods. Psyche understood that the goddess sought her death, and in fact she knew no other way than death to reach the underworld at all. Despairing then of any solution, she made her way slowly up a great tower, thinking to throw herself down from it and die. Once again, however, Cupid cared for her, and as she looked down on the green woods and valleys for the last time, a voice spoke to her out of the air saying, "Do not lose heart now, Psyche, for your trials are almost at an end. Go down to the hill of Tenaros, where yawns the mouth of a still, dark cave. Take with you two small copper coins in your mouth to give to Charon, one for the passage over the Styx and another to return. In each hand take a piece of bread scattered with barley meal and dipped in honey to throw to the great dog Cerberus who guards Hades' gate. Let nobody by the wayside tempt you to help him, lest you drop one of these. In order to deceive you, Aphrodite will cause shadowy figures to sit by the wayside begging aid, but pass them all by till you come to the house of Hades and do your errand. When Hades receives you there and would entertain you well, accept nothing that is offered but dry, brown bread. Do not sit in his chairs or join in his feasting, for if you do, you will never return. Only sit on the ground in front of him until the queen has filled your box. Take the box and return immediately, but be sure you do not open it as you come."

Psyche thanked the voice and did as it said. While

she felt her way down the grey and ghostly cavern, not
daring to put out her hands lest she drop the bread she
carried, an old man driving a donkey with a load of
sticks came to meet her up the path. As he turned aside
to give her room, the donkey slipped, and all the sticks
fell scattering and bouncing down the rocks. The poor
old man wrung his hands and hobbled about, trying to
gather them up and repack the donkey's load. But he
was lame and stiff so that he could not clamber, and he
prayed Psyche to help him. Then she remembered the
words of the voice and would not, but went on, though
the old man called piteously after her down the long,
dark road.

At last she came to the grey mud of the Styx and the
crowds of ghostly figures that eddied around its bank.
These fled aside as she approached them, shrieking on a
high, shrill note, and she passed through the lane they
made for her to the water's edge. Charon, the ferryman,
was old and bent and ragged, and he stood upright in
his ancient barge, leaning on a pole. His straggling
locks and beard and the clothes he wore were grey as
the river mud; only his eyes were red. He took the copper coin from Psyche's lips into one skinny hand and
without a word began to pole his boat slowly into the
middle of the stream. As they came out from the bank,
Psyche heard a dreadful cry from the black water and
saw an old man trying desperately to swim across and
holding up his hands in agony towards the barge. For-
getting what she held, she stretched out her hand to
him, then seeing the bread in it, she withdrew it just in

time. The old man gave a final cry and sank, but the barge moved on.

The dark, gleaming gates of Hades towered on the other side. Psyche cast a shuddering glance at the three-headed dog that growled before it, and threw him a piece of bread. He snapped at it angrily, snarling as he devoured it, but he made no move when Psyche slipped quickly past. Thus she came into the shadowy house and did all that the voice had commanded her, refusing food and entertainment, and asking only for the box filled with the beauty of Hades' queen. When she came out past Cerberus, she gave Charon the other coin, and then heard the sounds of wailing die down behind her as she clambered up the steep and rocky road. At last she stepped out of the mouth of the cavern into the brilliant sun and sat to rest in thankfulness for her escape. Here her eyes fell on the box of divine beauty that she carried in her hand, and she grudged Aphrodite its possession, saying to herself, "If I take a little of this beauty, will not Cupid find me fairer to look upon?" At this thought she opened the box and bent over it, but could see nothing therein. Only an oppressive and deadly scent came flowing out, until presently she felt her senses reeling and fell to the ground, stretched out in a death-like sleep.

There she might have slept forever, overcome by the beauty of the gods, had not Cupid been searching for her. He had been to the throne of Zeus and won consent to his marriage with Psyche. At last, therefore, he came to take her up to Olympus as his bride. He roused

Psyche and took away the deadly spell, restoring it to the box whence it had escaped. Then leading her by the hand, he brought her up to Olympus, where the gods received her royally. Zeus came out to meet her and presented her to Aphrodite, commanding the goddess to be reconciled. He handed to Psyche a golden cup. As she drank, the nectar of the gods coursed through her veins so that she was changed into an immortal. Finally in the palace of Olympus, Cupid and Psyche held their wedding feast. The Graces decked the hall with roses; the Muses lifted their lovely voices in a marriage song; Apollo played for their pleasure on his golden lyre; and to crown all in honor of the marriage, lovely, white-footed Aphrodite danced.

The Spring Flowers

The Greeks, who loved all beauty, loved especially the spring. Many were the legends they told of the countless flowers that blossomed on rocky mountain, rich slope, and fertile valley. The hyacinth, for instance, was once Hyacinthus, a beautiful boy with clustering locks. For his sake Apollo deserted the company of the gods and his oracle at Delphi to play in the hills and woods of the Spartan country in which Hyacinthus lived. So lovely was the boy that the West Wind, as it whistled through his curls, whispered to him to forsake Apollo and race with the wind on the hilltops. Since, however, Hyacinthus loved Apollo and would not listen, the jealous wind swore revenge.

One day Apollo and Hyacinthus chanced to be throwing the discus, which is a flat, heavy plate about a foot across. It is thrown with an underarm swing and goes spinning through the air. As Apollo and Hyacinthus played, Apollo cast the discus high and far. Hyacinthus, who was standing some way ahead to mark the spot where it should come down, rushed forward incautiously. At this moment the wind caught the flat, spinning discus and blew it to one side so that it struck Hyacinthus on the head, killing him instantly. Apollo grieved bitterly for the boy, but, god though he was, he could not raise him from the dead. Instead he changed him into a flower with bright, curling petals in memory of Hyacinthus' locks. Men said that if you looked at those petals carefully, you would see on them marks which spelled out AI AI, which means in Greek, "Alas!"

Narcissus was also a beautiful boy with whom many nymphs and maidens fell in love. Among these was the nymph, Echo, whom the goddess, Hera, had enchanted with a strange spell. Ever since then Echo could not talk. She could only answer by repeating the last words that others said. For a long time, therefore, poor Echo followed Narcissus about, unable to speak with him. Then one day as they were hunting, Narcissus became separated from his companions and began to call for them. "Is there anybody here?" he shouted.

"Here!" said Echo gladly.

"Come," cried Narcissus.

"Come!" she answered him.

"Here let us meet," called the boy.

"Let us meet," said Echo, but when she appeared, Narcissus cared nothing for her. So cold and cruel was he that the poor nymph crept away and hid herself that none might see her misery. She pined and wasted away for love until she faded quite from sight, so that now she is only a voice which still answers with the last words that you call.

The gods were angry with Narcissus for his cruel
treatment of Echo, and the more so because he was
proud and unkind to many other girls who were at-
tracted by his beauty. Therefore, to punish him, they
cast on him a terrible spell. There was a clear pool deep
in the woods to which no shepherds ever came. No bird
or beast or fallen branch ever disturbed its crystal waters. Through the woods came Narcissus one day, hot
and weary with hunting. He saw the gleaming silver
with a rim of green grass round and turned aside to refresh himself. He threw himself on the bank and put
down his face to the water, where he saw a most lovely
face upturned to his. He smiled at it in welcome. It
smiled lovingly back, but when he bent forward to kiss
it, it broke up into ripples at the touch of his lips. As he
started back, it reformed again and gazed at him with
longing. This time he stretched out one hand cautiously
and saw its hand stretched out to meet him, but his fingers touched only water; there was nothing there. In
despair Narcissus called to the shadow, in whispers at
first. Then as he saw it speaking, while yet he could
hear nothing, he called louder and louder. No one answered him but Echo, forlornly repeating his desperate
words of love.

For days Narcissus knelt by the pool, hopelessly in
love with the beauty of his own reflection. Before his
eyes he saw the image grow pale and thin, weep tears,
stretch out its arms, and look at him. Still he could not
hear it, could not touch it, no matter how he implored.

At last the gods took pity on his misery and changed him into a flower.

Adonis, like Persephone, was sometimes called the spirit of spring itself. He was a herdsman and a hunter, beloved by Aphrodite, who would often beg him to stay with her instead of hunting with his friends. She was timid, loving luxury and ease, and fearful for the safety of her favorites. Adonis, however, was a young and vigorous shepherd who enjoyed the hunt, and would not listen, until one day the fears of Aphrodite were cruelly realized. Adonis was slain by a boar while out hunting, and the queen of beauty was left disconsolate.

Aphrodite mourned Adonis bitterly. She came running through the thicket to where he lay and threw herself down by him, kissing him and crying. Out of his blood she made the red rose grow, and where her tears fell sprang up the anemone, which is called the windflower because the wind blows its petals so quickly. By the shortness of its life it recalls the young Adonis who died so early. Finally, Aphrodite and her attendants, the Graces, lifted Adonis up and laid him on a golden bier, anointing him with sweet scents, spreading over him a scarlet coverlet, and heaping him with flowers.

Many songs of lamentation were sung over Adonis, and the legend went that Aphrodite eventually won permission from Zeus to have Adonis back with her for six months of the year. For six months Adonis dwelt with Persephone in the land of the dead, and for six he returned to the goddess, and spring came on earth. In many cities there were spring festivals in honor of the marriage of Aphrodite and Adonis, where images of the two were laid together on a golden couch covered with a cloth stiff with precious embroidery. A singer would chant a marriage song, and all would celebrate the rebirth of Adonis and the coming of spring.

Eternal Youth

Eternal life and eternal youth are gifts men have always wanted, but to the Greeks these belonged to the gods alone, and very few mortals were ever granted them. There was an afterlife in Hades, but there men were poor, thin ghosts with bat-like, twittering voices and little power to enjoy or feel. Even Achilles, greatest of heroes, who lived in the land of the blessed dead among pleasant woods and meadows of daffodil, declared that he would rather be the meanest and most miserable slave on earth than the great prince of Hades that he was. Several stories are told of eternal youth and how hard it is to attain it. Among these are the love stories of Artemis, the moon huntress, and Eos, whom we know better by her Latin name of Aurora, goddess of the dawn.

In most legends Artemis is the shy huntress who chases the deer and the wild boar on the mountains with her silver bow. She loves the company of her nymphs alone and has sworn to keep away from man. One hunter, Actaeon, who spied on her as she was bathing, was even changed into a deer and run down by his own dogs as a punishment for his daring.

Yet there is a story that Artemis fell in love with Endymion, a shepherd who kept watch among the hills. Great was the love between the handsome, dark-eyed shepherd and the silver goddess who caressed him nightly with her beams. But since men grow sick and old while goddesses are forever young, Artemis could not possess Endymion always in the vigor of his youth. Therefore while he was still young, she sent upon him an enchanted sleep in which he might lie eternally, unheeding the lapse of time. In the shelter of a little cave on a high mountain side, on a couch of leaves and grass lies Endymion, sleeping forever, still rosy and youthful as in life. Month by month when the silver light of the full moon steals quietly in and caresses him, he smiles in his dream, and the moon goddess smiles at him and then passes silently on.

The love of Aurora for Tithonus was more tragic than this. Tithonus was a prince of Troy and marvelously handsome, so that the golden Dawn carried him away to her palace in the East, there to live with her in joy forever. She even went up to Olympus to ask Zeus for the gift of immortality for her love, but though Zeus consented to her prayer, she forgot to ask also for the gift of eternal youth. For a while the lovers lived in joy in the many-colored house of Aurora, which stood by the ocean shore at the farthest edge of the world. At last, however, the hair of Tithonus grew grey, then white; his face became furrowed and his limbs bowed. For a long time the goddess tended him carefully, though more like a daughter than a wife. Finally the wits of the poor, toothless old man began to fail him, and his trembling legs would no longer support his frame. Then the goddess lifted him gently up, laid him on a great bed in an inner room, and quietly closed the brazen doors.

There, one story says, he lies forever, each year a little weaker and more shrunken, babbling foolishly in a high quaver to himself. Some say, however, that he was changed into the grasshopper and that the little creature with the high, shrill voice and lean, shrunken limbs is all that is left of Tithonus, who was once beautiful and lived with the gods.

III

EARLY HISTORY
OF MANKIND

The Creation of Man

The Greeks have several stories about how man came to be. One declares that he was created in the age of Kronos, or Saturn, who ruled before Zeus. At that time, the legend says, there was no sorrow, toil, sickness, or age. Men lived their lives in plenty and died as though they went to sleep. They tilled no ground, built no cities, killed no living thing, and among them war was unknown. The earth brought forth strawberries, cherries, and ears of wheat for them. Even on the bramble bushes grew berries good to eat. Milk and sweet nectar flowed in rivers for men to drink, and honey dripped from hollow trees. Men lived in caves and thickets, needing little shelter, for the season was always spring.

Another legend declares that Zeus conceived of animals first and he entrusted their creation to Prometheus and Epimetheus, his brother. First, Epimetheus undertook to order all things, but he was a heedless person and soon got into trouble. Finally he was forced to appeal to Prometheus.

"What have you done?" asked Prometheus.

"Down on the earth," answered his brother, "there is a green, grassy clearing, ringed by tall oak trees and shaded by steep slopes from all but the midday sun. There I sat and the animals came to me, while I gave to each the gifts which should be his from this time forward. Air I gave to the birds, seas to the fishes, land to four-footed creatures and the creeping insects, and to some, like the moles, I gave burrows beneath the earth."

"That was well done," answered Prometheus. "What else did you do?"

"Strength," said Epimetheus, "I gave to lions and tigers, and the fierce animals of the woods. Size I gave to others like the great whales of the sea. The deer I made swift and timid, and the insects I made tiny that they might escape from sight. I gave warm fur to the great bears and the little squirrels, keen eyes and sharp talons to the birds of prey, tusks to the elephant, hide to the wild boar, sweet songs and bright feathers to the birds. To each I gave some special excellence, that whether large or small, kind or terrible, each might live in his own place, find food, escape enemies, and enjoy the wide world which is his to inhabit."

"All this is very good," said his brother, Prometheus. "You have done well. Wherein lies your trouble?"

"Because I did not think it out beforehand," said the heedless brother sadly, "I did not count how many animals there were to be before I started giving. Now when I have given all, there comes one last animal for whom I have neither skill nor shape, nor any place to dwell in. Everything has been given already."

"What is this animal," said Prometheus, "who has been forgotten?"

"His name," said Epimetheus, "is Man."

Thus it was that the future of man was left to Prometheus, who was forced to make man different from all other creatures. Therefore he gave him the shape of the gods themselves and the privilege of walking upright as they do. He gave him no special home, but made him ruler over the whole earth, and over the sea and air. Finally, he gave him no special strength or swiftness, but stole a spark from heaven and lighted a heavenly fire within his mind which should teach him to understand, to count, to speak, to remember. Man learned from it how to build cities, tame animals, raise crops, build boats, and do all the things that animals cannot. Prometheus also kindled fire on earth that man might smelt metals and make tools. In fact, from this heavenly fire of Prometheus all man's greatness comes.

Before this time fire was a divine thing and belonged only to the gods. It was one of their greatest treasures, and Zeus would never have given Prometheus permission to use it in the creation of man. Therefore when Prometheus stole it, Zeus was furious indeed. He chained Prometheus to a great, lofty rock, where the sun scorched him by day and the cruel frost tortured him by night. Not content with that, he sent an eagle to tear him, so that, though he could not die, he lived in agony. For many centuries Prometheus hung in torment, but he was wiser than Zeus, and by reason of a secret he had, he forced Zeus in later ages to set him free. By then, also, Zeus had learned that there is more in ruling than power and cruelty. Thus, the two at last were friends.

The Coming of Evil

After the punishment of Prometheus, Zeus planned to take his revenge on man. He could not recall the gift of fire, since it had been given by one of the immortals, but he was not content that man should possess this treasure in peace and become perhaps as great as were the gods themselves. He therefore took counsel with the other gods, and together they made for man a woman. All the gods gave gifts to this new creation. Aphrodite gave her fresh beauty like the spring itself. The goddess Athene dressed her and put on her a garland of flowers and green leaves. She had also a golden diadem beautifully decorated with figures of animals. In her heart Hermes put cunning, deceit, and curiosity. She was named Pandora, which means All-Gifted, since each of the gods had given her something. The last gift was a chest in which there was supposed to be great treasure, but which Pandora was instructed never to open. Then Hermes, the Messenger, took the girl and brought her to Epimetheus.

Epimetheus had been warned by his brother to receive no gifts from Zeus, but he was a heedless person, as ever, and Pandora was very lovely. He accepted her, therefore, and for a while they lived together in happiness, for Pandora besides her beauty had been given both wit and charm. Eventually, however, her curiosity got the better of her, and she determined to see for herself what treasure it was that the gods had given her. One day when she was alone, she went over to the corner where her chest lay and cautiously lifted the lid for a peep. The lid flew up out of her hands and knocked her aside, while before her frightened eyes dreadful, shadowy shapes flew out of the box in an endless stream. There were hunger, disease, war, greed, anger, jealousy, toil, and all the griefs and hardships to which man from that day has been subject. Each was terrible in appearance, and as it passed, Pandora saw something of the misery that her thoughtless action had brought on her descendants. At last the stream slackened, and Pandora, who had been paralyzed with fear and horror, found strength to shut her box. The only thing left in it now, however, was the one good gift the gods had put in among so many evil ones. This was hope, and since that time the hope that is in man's heart is the only thing which has made him able to bear the sorrows that Pandora brought upon him.

The Great Flood

When evil first came among mankind, people became very wicked. War, robbery, treachery, and murder prevailed throughout the world. Even the worship of the gods, the laws of truth and honor, reverence for parents and brotherly love were neglected.

Finally, Zeus determined to destroy the race of men altogether, and the other gods agreed. All the winds were therefore shut up in a cave except the South Wind, the wet one. He raced over the earth with water streaming from his beard and long, white hair. Clouds gathered around his head, and dew dripped from his wings and the ends of his garments. With him went Iris, the rainbow goddess, while below Poseidon smote the earth with his trident until it shook and gaped open, so that the waters of the sea rushed up over the land.

Fields and farmhouses were buried. Fish swam in the tops of the trees. Sea beasts were quietly feeding where flocks and herds had grazed before. On the surface of the water, boars, stags, lions, and tigers struggled desperately to keep afloat. Wolves swam in the midst of flocks of sheep, but the sheep were not frightened by them, and the wolves never thought of their natural prey. Each fought for his own life and forgot the others. Over them wheeled countless birds, winging far and wide in the hope of finding something to rest upon. Eventually they too fell into the water and were drowned.

All over the water were men in small boats or makeshift rafts. Some even had oars which they tried to use, but the waters were fierce and stormy, and there was nowhere to go. In time all were drowned, until at last there was no one left but an old man and his wife, Deucalion and Pyrrha. These two people had lived in truth and justice, unlike the rest of mankind. They had been warned of the coming of the flood and had built a boat and stocked it. For nine days and nights they floated until Zeus took pity on them and they came to the top of Mount Parnassus, the sacred home of the Muses. There they found land and disembarked to wait while the gods recalled the water they had unloosed.

When the waters fell, Deucalion and Pyrrha looked over the land, despairing. Mud and sea slime covered the earth; all living things had been swept away. Slowly and sadly they made their way down the mountain until they came to a temple where there had been an oracle. Black seaweed dripped from the pillars now, and the mud was over all. Nevertheless the two knelt down and kissed the temple steps while Deucalion prayed to the goddess to tell them what they should do. All men were dead but themselves, and they were old. It was impossible that they should have children to people the earth again. Out of the temple a great voice was heard speaking strange words.

"Depart," it said, "with veiled heads and loosened robes, and throw behind you as you go the bones of your mother."

Pyrrha was in despair when she heard this saying. "The bones of our mother!" she cried. "How can we tell now where they lie? Even if we knew, we could never do such a dreadful thing as to disturb their resting place and scatter them over the earth like an armful of stones."

"Stones!" said Deucalion quickly. "That must be what the goddess means. After all Earth is our mother, and the other thing is too horrible for us to suppose that a goddess would ever command it."

Accordingly both picked up armfuls of stones, and as they went away from the temple with faces veiled, they cast the stones behind them. From each of those Deucalion cast sprang up a man, and from Pyrrha's stones sprang women. Thus the earth was repeopled, and in the course of time it brought forth again animals from itself, and all was as before. Only from that time men have been less sensitive and have found it easier to endure toil, and sorrow, and pain, since now they are descended from stones.

IV

MEN'S RIVALRY
WITH GODS

Niobe

Pride and haughtiness against the gods were greater offences than any men could commit against one another. Mortals needed to remember that they were inferior beings, neither all powerful nor all wise, and that they owed worship and honor to the immortals, who were far greater than themselves. Greek legend has many stories of heroes who, because of their birth or their wisdom or their daring, sought to have power and worship that was given only to the divine. The vengeance of the gods was swift, that men might learn to know the limitations of their nature.

It was the festival of Leto in the city of Thebes, and all the mothers of the city were making a great procession to her temple, with incense in their hands and wreaths of laurel in honor of the divine mother who bore the twins, Artemis and Apollo. Though the song of the worshippers was loud, however, there was an air of uneasiness over the procession. The watching crowds were murmuring to one another; many an anxious eye was cast at the royal palace, past which the winding train must go. For Niobe, proudest and haughtiest of the women of Greece, was not with the worshipers, though both as queen and as mother her place was with the foremost of all.

To tell the truth, the citizens of Thebes were somewhat frightened of their lordly mistress, who was so rich, so nobly born, and so successful in everything she undertook. It was said her father, Tantalus, had been a friend of Zeus and had even been admitted to Olympus to dine at the tables of the gods. There he had dared to fall in love with Hera, the queen of heaven, and had been dreadfully punished for his insolence. Yet in a sense the very loftiness of his ambition caused his memory to be held in awe. Nor was this all. Tantalus had the name of being a son of Zeus, while Niobe's mother was a daughter of Atlas, the great giant who holds up the sky.

Ever since Niobe had come to Thebes, she had held herself apart. Did not the blood of immortals run in her veins? Was she not queen? Was she not divinely tall and fair? Had she not seven sons and seven daughters, the like of whose vigor and beauty had never been seen? None of the gods could boast a family such as hers. Niobe even grudged the gods their worship because like honor was not paid to her. She had let it be known that any who sought her favor had best not be seen presenting offerings at the temples. The citizens had respected her wishes, not daring to do otherwise, but they had been uneasy. Sure enough some days before, the city had been awakened by the cry of a prophetess in the streets at early dawn.

"Women of Thebes," she was calling, "awake! awake! The altars of Leto are cold, her shrines and temples bare. Awake and do honor to the mother of the terrible twin gods, lest arrows of death smite you from the gold or silver bow."

People thronged the streets to hear the prophetess, consulting with one another in low voices. On the whole it seemed to them better to brave the anger of Niobe than that of Leto. Moreover, they hoped that Niobe would refuse the direct challenge of the goddess and let the festival take place. All, therefore, was put in readiness. Temples were decorated with laurel, and now on the appointed day the procession of worshipers actually went winding past the palace gates.

Outside the palace the crowd of onlookers was thickest, though their eyes were more on the great bronze doors than on the head of the advancing procession. Sure enough the doors were opening. White-clad slaves were holding them apart, while between them, followed by an imposing array of guards and rich attendants, Niobe came out to meet the worshipers. The uneasy murmurs hushed as she approached, while the head of the procession halted, bumped into from behind in an undignified way. The singing died out, and the two parties stood looking at one another for a moment. Very stately was Niobe in scarlet and gold, with her fair hair falling on her shoulders from beneath a tall, embroidered headdress. Her voice was raised, distinct and haughty, so that in the sudden silence it carried far.

"Who is Leto," she demanded, "that you worship

her? Do you bring incense to my altars? I, too, am a
child of gods. Moreover I am a great queen among you
on earth. Leto wandered over all the world to find
a resting place, and none would receive her but the
rocky island of Delos. On that barren land the poor exile gave birth to two children. Yet she is honored as
most blessed of mothers, while I, the great queen, the
god-descended, have borne seven times as many, each
one of them as fair. Go home and think things over. Let
me not see again that Leto is honored until I am honored first."

People were frightened at Niobe's words. Some even
looked angry, but the armed guards were fierce and nobody wanted a fight. There was confusion as the
procession broke up, but little talk within sight of
Niobe's eyes. Only the laurel wreaths were not thrown
down, but taken quietly and soberly home. That night
the temple of Leto was heaped with shining branches as
people with faces hidden stole secretly inside and laid
them there.

The vengeance of the gods was not long in coming.
Apollo was the first to listen to the complaint of outraged Leto, and when morning came he sped down
from Olympus swift as a ray of light. The golden arrows that never miss their mark rattled in his quiver as
he came. Niobe's seven sons were in the meadowland
outside the city, practicing riding, and wrestling, and
various other sports. Suddenly the eldest son, who was
leading in the horse race, threw up his arms and fell
headlong, while the second, frantically reining in his

horse, pitched forward over its head onto his brother's corpse. Two, who were wrestling, Phoebus hit with a single arrow and killed in each other's arms. One ran to lift them and fell dead likewise. Another minute and the sixth was slain, while the youngest one shrieked so piteously to the unseen archer that he might have spared him, but it was too late. The arrow was already loosed which stretched him with his brothers.

Terrible was the outcry in the city and bitter the grief of the seven sisters of the dead. Only Niobe in the midst of her sorrow was angry. Raising herself from the dead bodies of her sons, she cried to Leto, "These you have slain by treachery, but my daughters I shall keep by me. Still I am greater than you are, in that you have but two children while I have seven."

Thus she spoke in the palace as the sun went down, and she and her daughters clad in black stood over the scarlet-covered biers of the dead. Presently, however, the silver moon stole through the doorway, and the eldest sister fell dead without a sound across her brothers' bodies. Before any could move, the second fell, and with that the group broke up shrieking, to drop even as they fled or cowered in corners to escape the pitiless arrows. The poor mother seized the youngest in her arms, bending over her and trying to shield the little girl's body with her own, while she piteously begged Artemis to spare her this last one. Again the unseen bowstring twanged, and the little body that clung to Niobe twitched suddenly and went limp. The mother set her down and sat down herself in the midst of the hall, too proud to hide her head or to say anything of her sorrow. Only as she looked at the bodies of her children strewn about her, tears rolled from her great, blue eyes and over her pale cheeks, but she neither moved nor said a word.

Niobe's unhappy husband killed himself from grief, but the queen heard nothing of it, or at least she made no sign. Still she sat deaf and motionless with the slow tears rolling down her cheeks until she seemed to her helpless attendants turned to stone. Even the gods pitied her at last and turned her to stone in actual fact. They set her on a mountain in Phrygia near the place where she was born. There forever Niobe sits, weeping two streams of water in silent memory of her dead.

Daedalus

In the very early days it was not the mainland of Greece that was the most important, but the island of Crete, which lies below the Aegean sea, south of most of the other islands. In it there are still ruins of a great palace, almost more a city than a palace, with so many rooms and passages that it must have had many people dwelling in it. These people were evidently traders and powerful on the sea. They must have been skilled ship-builders, and from the remains we have found, we know they were also great architects, craftsmen, and artists. In later times the island sank into unimportance, and its former prominence was forgotten. Nevertheless the story of its greatness lingers on and is associated with the skills for which we know it was famous.

In legend the king of the island of Crete was called Minos. He had a great fleet and power that extended far and wide, dominating, among other places, the city of Athens. He seems to have been a fierce tyrant, for he forced the Athenians to send him a yearly tribute of seven youths and seven maidens, whom he fed to a horrible monster that he owned. This animal was called the Minotaur and was a creature with the head of a bull and the body of a man. To keep him safe and to prevent his victims from escaping, it was necessary to build him some special dwelling. For this purpose Minos hired a famous architect whose name was Daedalus.

Daedalus, the Greeks used to say, was the first great artist, craftsman, and engineer. It was he who invented many of the tools of carpentry: the saw, the gimlet, and an efficient glue. He also was the first to make statues more lifelike than a roughly carved pillar. Before this time statues had held their legs stiffly together and their arms down by their sides. Daedalus made them stepping forward and holding something in front of them. He is said to have built a great reservoir, fortified a city, and done many other engineering works. But the most famous of all the things he made was the house he built for Minos to keep the Minotaur in. This house was a labyrinth or maze, with countless winding passages, so that it was hard to find the way in or out. Perhaps the idea got into the story from a vague memory of the countless confusing passages in the Cretan palace. In any case Daedalus is supposed to have built a maze for Minos, so elaborate in its windings that no man without a clue could possibly escape from it.

Minos was delighted with his labyrinth and held the architect in great honor. Unfortunately when the wandering artist wished to take his fee and go, the king had other ideas. There were many things that could well be made for him by the greatest craftsman in the world, and he saw no reason why he should let the man build things for someone else. Being king over an island, Minos found it easy to keep Daedalus where he was. He simply forbade all ships to give the artist passage, provided him with an elaborate workshop, and suggested that he might as well settle down and be happy.

Thus Minos gained the services of Daedalus, but the great craftsman was not content. Beyond anything else he loved freedom to wander as he pleased, seeing the world and picking up new ideas. He was not the kind of man who could easily settle down. Therefore when he saw that he could not possibly get away by ship, he turned his talents to working out something else. Minos did not visit the fine workshop he had given his artist, but if he had, he would have seen a curious sight. The whole place was deep in feathers. There were feathers of all shapes and sizes, some just thrown down anyhow as they had been brought in, and some neatly sorted into heaps. A young boy, Icarus, Daedalus' only son and companion, was doing the sorting, while Daedalus himself was busy with twine, wax, and glue, fixing the feathers together in orderly rows on a wooden framework.

Daedalus was making wings. He had seen that it would be impossible to cross the sea by boat because of Minos' order, so he had determined to fly across it. After studying the wings of birds for a long time, he designed some which he thought would support a man, and now he was working on them. Icarus was terribly excited and was helping eagerly. He did not so much dislike living in Crete, but he wanted to fly as the gods do. Think of being the first man to have wings!

The wings took a long time to finish, but at last they were done, a mighty pair for Daedalus, and a smaller one for his son. The workshop being in the top of a lofty tower, Daedalus planned that they should simply launch themselves into the air from it. As they stood there, fastening the wings onto their shoulders, Daedalus gave his excited son some last instructions.

"I shall go first," he said, "to show the way. We must go straight across the sea by the shortest route, lest we become tired and drown before we can reach land. Follow me, and remember the wings on your shoulders are not natural wings, like those of Cupid. We are men and must use tools to do what the gods can do for themselves. Even with our tools we must always fall short of them. If you fly too near the sea, the feathers will become wet and heavy, and you will drown; if you fly up into the air as the gods do, the wax will melt in the sun long before you reach Olympus. Then your wings will fall off and you will perish. Follow me as I go through the middle of the air, neither too high nor too low. So you will be safe."

He spoke and jumped, falling like a stone till the wind caught him and he steadied. Then he began to rise again as the wings beat steadily from his shoulders. He turned and beckoned Icarus to come on. Icarus jumped.

The fall was terrible; so was the sudden stop as his spread wings caught the air. Still, he had the presence of mind to work his arms as he had seen his father do, and pretty soon he was sailing ahead in long swoops over the sea.

Presently the boy began to play tricks in the air. His father flew steadily on, but it would be easy, Icarus thought, to catch up with him. Father was too old to enjoy this properly. The swoops were rather sickening, but climbing was wonderful. Up, up he went, like the lark, like the eagle, like the gods. His father called something, but the wind whistled the sound away. Icarus realized he ought to come down, but nobody had ever been up there before, except the gods. Perhaps the real difference between gods and men was that gods could fly. If he wanted to reach Olympus, he would have to take some risk.

Up, up Icarus went, soaring into the bright sun. In vain Daedalus called to him. He was only a black speck by now. At last he was coming down. He was coming very fast, much too fast. In another second Daedalus caught sight of the boy, whirling headlong. The framework was still on his shoulders, but the feathers had all fallen off, as the hot sun had melted the wax. One moment he saw him; then with a mighty splash Icarus hit the water and was gone. Daedalus circled round over the sea, not daring to go too low lest his own wings become soaked. There was no point in both being drowned. But not even a clutching hand broke surface.

The white foam hung on the water for a space; then it too disappeared.

Daedalus flew on. He reached the land at last, white-faced and exhausted, but he would neither use his wings nor teach others how to make them. He had learned man's limitations. It is not right for him to soar like the gods.

Midas

Midas was king in Phrygia, which is a land in Asia
Minor, and he was both powerful and rich.
Nevertheless he was foolish, obstinate, and hasty, with-
out the sense to appreciate good advice.

It happened one time that Dionysus with his dancing nymphs and satyrs passed through Phrygia. As they
went, the old, fat Silenus nodding on his ass strayed
from the others, who danced on without missing him.
The ass took his half-conscious master wherever he
wanted, until some hours later as they came to a great
rose garden, the old man tumbled off. The king's gar-
deners found him there and roused him, still sleepy and
staggering, not quite sure who or where he was. Since,
however, the revels of Dionysus had spread throughout
the land, they recognized him as the god's companion
and made much of him. They wreathed his neck with
roses and, one on each side and one behind, they supported him to the palace and up the steps, while
another went to fetch Midas.

The king came out to meet Silenus, overjoyed at the
honor done him. He clapped his hands for his servants

and demanded such a feast as never was. There was much running to and fro and setting up of tables, fetching of wine, and bringing up of sweet scented oil. While slaves festooned the hall with roses and made garlands for the feasters, Midas conducted his guest to the bath with all honor, that he might refresh himself and put on clean garments for the feast.

A magnificent celebration followed. For ten days by daylight and by torchlight the palace of the king stood open, and all the notables of Phrygia came up and down its steps. There was sound of lyre and pipe, and singing. There was dancing. Everywhere the scent of roses and of wine mingled with the costly perfumes of King Midas in the hot summer air. In ten days' time, as the revels were dying down from sheer exhaustion, Dionysus came in person to seek his friend. When he found how Silenus had been entertained and honored, he was greatly pleased and promised Midas any gift he cared to name, no matter what it was.

The king thought a little, glancing back through his doors at the chaos in his hall of scattered rose petals, overturned tables, bowls for the wine-mixing, and drinking cups. It had been a good feast, the sort of feast a king should give, only he was very weary now and could not think. A king should entertain thus and give kingly presents to his guests, cups of beaten gold, such as he had seen once with lifelike pictures of a hunt running round them, or the golden honeycomb which Daedalus made exactly as though it were the work of bees. Gods like these guests should have golden statues. Even a king never had enough.

"Give me," he said to Dionysus suddenly, "the power to turn all I touch to gold."

"That is a rash thing to ask," said Dionysus solemnly. "Think again." But eastern kings are never contradicted, and Midas only felt annoyed.

"It is my wish," he answered coldly.

Dionysus nodded. "You shall have it," he said. "As you part from me here in the garden, it shall be yours."

Midas was so excited when he came back through the garden that he could not make up his mind what to touch first. Presently he decided on the branch of an oak tree which overhung his path. He took a look at it first, counting the leaves, noticing the little veins in them, the jagged edges, the fact that one of them had been eaten half away. He put out his hand to break it off. He never saw it change. One moment it was brown and green; the next it wasn't. There it was, stiff and shining, nibbled leaf and all. It was hard and satisfyingly heavy and more natural far than anything Daedalus ever made.

Now he was the greatest king in the world. Midas looked down at the grass he was walking over. It was still green; the touch was evidently in his hands. He picked up a stone to see; it became a lump of gold. He tried a clod of earth and found himself with another lump. Midas was beside himself with joy; he went into his palace to see what he could do. In the doorway he stopped at a sudden thought. He went outside again

and walked down all the long row of pillars, laying his
hands on each one. No king in the world had pillars of
solid gold. He considered having a gold house but re-
jected the idea; the gold pillars looked better against the
stone. Midas picked a gold apple and went inside again
to eat.

His servants set his table for him, and he amused
himself by turning the cups and dishes into gold. He
touched the table too by mistake — not that it really
mattered, but he would have to be careful. Absently he
picked up a piece of bread and bit it and nearly broke
his teeth. Midas sat with the golden bread in his hand
and looked at it a long time. He was horribly frightened. "I shall have to eat it without touching it with my
hands," he said to himself after a while, and he put his
head down on the table and tried that way. It was no
good. The moment his lips touched the bread, he felt it
turn hard and cold. In his shock he groped wildly for
his winecup and took a big gulp. The stuff flowed into
his mouth all right, but it wasn't wine any more. He
spat it out hastily before he choked himself. This time
he was more than frightened; he was desperate. "Great
Dionysus," he prayed earnestly with uplifted hands,
"forgive my foolishness and take away your gift."

"Go to the mountain of Tmolus," said the voice of
the god in his ear, "and bathe in the stream that springs
there so that the golden touch may be washed away.
The next time think more carefully before you set your
judgment against that of the gods."

Midas thanked the god with his whole heart, but he

paid more attention to his promise than to his advice. He lost no time in journeying to the mountain and dipping himself in the stream. There the golden touch was washed away from Midas, but the sand of the river bottom shone bright gold as the power passed into the water, so that the stream flowed over golden sand from that time on.

Midas had learned his lesson in a way, but was still conceited. He had realized at least that gold was not the most important thing. Indeed, having had too much gold at one time, he took a violent dislike to it and to luxury in general. He spent his time in the open country now, listening to the music of the streams and the woodlands, while his kingdom ran itself as best it might. He wanted neither his elaborate palace, his embroidered robes, his splendid feasts, nor his trained dancers and musicians. Instead he wished to be at home in the woodlands with simple things which were natural and unspoiled.

It happened at the time that in the woods of Tmolus the goat god Pan had made himself a pipe. It was a simple hollow reed with holes for stops cut in it, and the god played simple tunes on it like bird calls and the various noises of the animals he had heard. Only he was very skillful and could play them fast and slow, mixed together or repeated, until the listener felt that the woods themselves were alive with little creatures. The birds and beasts made answer to the pipe so that it seemed the whole wood was an orchestra of music. Midas himself was charmed to ecstasy with the beauty of it, and begged the shaggy god to play hour by hour till the very birds were weary of the calls. This Pan was quite ready to do, since he was proud of his invention. He even wanted to challenge Apollo himself, sure that any judge would put his instrument above Apollo's golden lyre.

Apollo accepted the challenge, and Tmolus, the mountain, was himself to be the judge. Tmolus was naturally a woodland god and friendly to Pan, so he listened with solemn pleasure as the pipe trilled airs more varied and more natural than it had ever played before. The woods echoed, and the happy Midas, who had followed Pan to the contest, was almost beside himself with delight at the gaiety and abandon of it all. When, however, Tmolus heard Apollo play the music of gods and heroes, of love, longing, heroism, and the mighty dead, he forgot his own woods around him, and the animals listening in their tiny nests and holes. He seemed to see into the hearts of men and understand the pity of their lives and the beauty that they longed for.

Even after the song had died away, Tmolus sat there in forgetful silence with his thoughts on the loves and struggles of the ages and the half-dried tears on his cheeks. There was a great quiet around him too, he realized, as he came to his senses. Even Pan had put down his pipe thoughtfully on the grass.

Tmolus gave the prize to Apollo, and in the whole woodland there was no one to protest but Midas. Midas had shut his ears to Apollo; he would neither listen nor care. Now he forgot where he was and in whose presence. All he remembered was that he was a great king who always gave his opinion and who, his courtiers told him, was always right. Leaping up, he protested loudly to Tmolus and was not even quiet when the mountain silently frowned on him. Getting no answer, he turned to Apollo, still objecting furiously to the unfairness of the judgment.

Apollo looked the insistent mortal up and down. "The fault is in your ears, O king. We must give them their true shape," he said. With that he turned away and was gone to Olympus, while the unfortunate Midas put his hands to his ears and found them long and furry. He could even wriggle them about. Apollo had given him asses' ears in punishment for his folly.

From that time on King Midas wore a scarlet turban and tried to make it seem as though wearing this were a privilege that only the king could enjoy. He wore it day and night, he was so fond of it. Presently, however, his hair began to grow so long and straggly that something had to be done. The royal barber had to be called.

The barber of King Midas was a royal slave, so it was easy enough to threaten him with the most horrible punishment if, whether waking or sleeping, he ever let fall the slightest hint of what was wrong with the king. The barber was thoroughly frightened. Unfortunately he was too frightened, and the king's threats preyed on his mind. He began to dream he had told his secret to somebody, and what was worse, his fellow servants began to complain that he was making noises in his sleep, so that he was desperately afraid he would talk. At last it seemed that if he could only tell somebody once and get it over, his mind would be at rest. Yet tell somebody was just what he dared not do. Finally, he went down to a meadow which was seldom crossed because it was waterlogged, and there, where he could see there was no one round to hear him, he dug a hole in the ground, put his face close down, and whispered into the wet mud, "King Midas has asses' ears." Then he threw some earth on top and went away, feeling somehow much relieved.

Nothing happened for a while except that the hole filled up with water. Presently, though, some reeds began to grow in it. They grew taller and rustled as the wind went through them. After a while someone happened to go down that way and came racing back, half amused and half terrified. Everyone crowded round to listen to him. It was certainly queer, but it was a bit amusing too.

Everybody streamed down the path to investigate. Sure enough, as they came close to it, they could hear the whole thing distinctly. The reeds were not rustling in the wind; they were whispering to one another, "King Midas has asses' ears . . . asses' ears . . . asses' ears."

V

LOVE STORIES OF THE HEROES

The Great Musician

In the legend of Orpheus the Greek love of music found its fullest expression. Orpheus, it is said, could make such heavenly songs that when he sat down to sing, the trees would crowd around to shade him. The ivy and vine stretched out their tendrils. Great oaks would bend their spreading branches over his head. The very rocks would edge down the mountainsides. Wild beasts crouched harmless by him, and nymphs and woodland gods would listen to him enchanted.

Orpheus himself, however, had eyes for no one but the nymph, Eurydice. His love for her was his inspiration, and his power sprang from the passionate longing that he knew in his own heart. All nature rejoiced with him on his bridal day, but on that very morning, as Eurydice went down to the riverside with her maidens to gather flowers for a bridal garland, she was bitten in the foot by a snake, and she died in spite of all attempts to save her.

Orpheus was inconsolable. All day long he mourned his bride, while birds, beasts, and the earth itself sorrowed with him. When at last the shadows of the sun

grew long, Orpheus took his lyre and made his way to the yawning cave which leads down into the underworld, where the soul of dead Eurydice had gone.

Even grey Charon, the ferryman of the Styx, forgot to ask his passenger for the price of crossing. The dog, Cerberus, the three-headed monster who guards Hades' gate, stopped full in his tracks and listened motionless until Orpheus had passed. As he entered the land of Hades, the pale ghosts came after him like great, uncounted flocks of silent birds. All the land lay hushed as that marvelous voice resounded across the mud and marshes of its dreadful rivers. In the daffodil fields of Elysium the happy dead sat silent among their flowers. In the farthest corners of the place of punishment, the hissing flames stood still. Accursed Sisyphus, who toils eternally to push a mighty rock uphill, sat down and knew not he was resting. Tantalus, who strains forever after visions of cool water, forgot his thirst and ceased to clutch at the empty air.

The pillared hall of Hades opened before the hero's song. The ranks of long-dead heroes who sit at Hades' board looked up and turned their eyes away from the pitiless form of Hades and his pale, unhappy queen. Grim and unmoving sat the dark king of the dead on his ebony throne, yet the tears shone on his rigid cheeks in the light of his ghastly torches. Even his hard heart, which knew all misery and cared nothing for it, was touched by the love and longing of the music.

At last the minstrel came to an end, and a long sigh like wind in pine trees was heard from the assembled ghosts. Then the king spoke, and his deep voice echoed through his silent land. "Go back to the light of day," he said. "Go quickly while my monsters are stilled by your song. Climb up the steep road to daylight, and never once turn back. The spirit of Eurydice shall follow, but if you look around at her, she will return to me."

Orpheus turned and strode from the hall of Hades, and the flocks of following ghosts made way for him to pass. In vain he searched their ranks for a sight of his lost Eurydice. In vain he listened for the faintest sound behind. The barge of Charon sank to the very gunwales beneath his weight, but no following passenger pressed it lower down. The way from the land of Hades to the upper world is long and hard, far easier to descend than climb. It was dark and misty, full of strange shapes and noises, yet in many places merely black and silent as the tomb. Here Orpheus would stop and listen, but nothing moved behind him. For all he could hear, he was utterly alone. Then he would wonder if the pitiless Hades were deceiving him. Suppose he came up to the light again and Eurydice was not there! Once he had charmed the ferryman and the dreadful monsters, but now they had heard his song. The second time his spell would be less powerful; he could never go again. Perhaps he had lost Eurydice by his readiness to believe.

Every step he took, some instinct told him that he was going farther from his bride. He toiled up the path in reluctance and despair, stopping, listening, sighing, taking a few slow steps, until the dark thinned out into greyness. Up ahead a speck of light showed clearly the entrance to the cavern.

At that final moment Orpheus could bear no more. To go out into the light of day without his love seemed to him impossible. Before he had quite ascended, there was still a moment in which he could go back. Quick in the greyness he turned and saw a dim shade at his heels, as indistinct as the grey mist behind her. But still he could see the look of sadness on her face as he sprung forward saying, "Eurydice!" and threw his arms about her. The shade dissolved in the circle of his arms like smoke. A little whisper seemed to say, "Farewell," as she scattered into mist and was gone.

The unfortunate lover hastened back again down the steep, dark path. But all was in vain. This time the ghostly ferryman was deaf to his prayers. The very wildness of his mood made it impossible for him to attain the beauty of his former music. At last, his despair was so great that he could not even sing at all. For seven days he sat huddled together on the grey mud banks, listening to the wailing of the terrible river. The flitting ghosts shrank back in a wide circle from the living man, but he paid them no attention. Only he sat with his eyes on Charon, his ears ringing with the dreadful noise of Styx.

Orpheus arose at last and stumbled back along the steep road he knew so well by now. When he came up to earth again, his song was pitiful but more beautiful than ever. Even the nightingale who mourned all night long would hush her voice to listen as Orpheus sat in some hidden place singing of his lost Eurydice. Men and women he could bear no longer, and when they came to hear him, he drove them away. At last the women of Thrace, maddened by Dionysus and infuriated by Orpheus' contempt, fell upon him and killed him. It is said that as the body was swept down the river Hebrus, the dead lips still moved faintly and the rocks echoed for the last time, "Eurydice." But the poet's eager spirit was already far down the familiar path.

In the daffodil meadows he met the shade of Eurydice, and there they walk together, or where the path is narrow, the shade of Orpheus goes ahead and looks back at his love.

The Lover of Beauty

Pygmalion was a sculptor, a worker in marble, bronze, and ivory. He was so young and handsome that the girls as they went past his workshop used to look in and admire him, hoping that he would notice them. But Pygmalion was devoted only to his art. People seemed noisy and trivial to him, and ugly too, for he had an image of beauty in his mind which caused him to work over his statues from morning to night, smoothing, re-working, always in search of a loveliness beyond his powers of expression. In truth the statues of Pygmalion were far more beautiful than human beings, and each statue was more nearly perfect than the last. Still in every one Pygmalion felt that there was something lacking. While others would stand entranced before them, he never cared to look on anything he had finished, but was immediately absorbed in the next attempt.

At last, however, he was working on an ivory statue of a girl in which he seemed to have expressed his ideal in every way. Even before it was done, he would lay down the chisel and stare at his work for an hour or so together, tracing in his mind the beauty that was as yet

111

only half unfolded. By the time the statue was nearly finished, Pygmalion could think of nothing else. In his very dreams the statue haunted him. Then she seemed to wake up for him and come alive. The idea gave him exquisite pleasure, and he used to dwell on it. The dreams passed into daydreams until for many days Pygmalion made little progress on his almost-finished statue. He would sit gazing at the maiden, whom he had christened Galatea, and imagining that perhaps he saw her move and the joy it would be if she actually were living. He became pale and exhausted; his dreams wore him out.

At last, the statue was actually finished. The slightest touch of the chisel now would be a change for the worse. Half the night Pygmalion gazed at the beautiful image; then with a hopeless sigh he went to bed, pursued as ever by his dreams. The next day he arose early, for he had something to do. It was the festival of Aphrodite, the goddess of beauty, to whom Pygmalion, since he was a seeker after beauty, had always felt a special devotion. Never once had he failed to give Aphrodite every possible honor that was due to her. In truth, his whole life was lived in worship of the goddess. There were many splendid gifts being given her, snow-white bulls with their horns covered with gold, wine, oil, and incense, embroidered garments, carvings, offerings of gold and ivory. Both rich and poor came in turn to offer their gifts. As he approached the altar, Pygmalion prayed earnestly and saw the fire that burned there leap suddenly in flame. Tense excitement stirred him; he could stay no longer; he must get back to his statue, though he did not quite know what he expected there. Galatea was as he had left her. He looked at her longingly once more, and again as he so often had, he seemed to see her stir. It was only a trick of imagination, he knew, because it had happened many times to him before. Nevertheless, on a sudden impulse, he went over to Galatea and took her in his arms.

The statue really was moving! He felt the hard ivory grow soft and warm like wax in his clasp. He saw the lips grow red and the cheeks blush faintly pink. Unbelieving he took her hand and lifted it. As he pressed it, he felt the fingers gently tighten in his own. Galatea opened her eyes and looked at him. There was understanding in her gaze. The red lips parted slightly, and as Pygmalion kissed them, they pressed against his own. Galatea stepped down from her pedestal into Pygmalion's arms a living girl. The next day two lovers went to pray at Aphrodite's shrine, the one thanking her for the gift of life, the other that his dreams and prayers had been answered and his lifelong devotion to the goddess thus rewarded.

The Fortunate King

Admetus, king of Pherae in Thessaly, was thought by many to be among the luckiest of men. He was young, strong, and handsome, the only son of a father who had given up the kingdom to him as soon as he came of age. Admetus was an affectionate son, and the old people felt proud and pleased that, though they had given him all their power, he still paid them every attention which could make their old age a happy one. Nor was this all. The wealth of the king lay largely in his immense flocks and herds, for which he had the good fortune to obtain a marvelous herdsman.

Apollo himself had been condemned to spend a year on earth in the form of a servant as a punishment for an offense he had committed in anger against Zeus. He came in this way to Admetus, and since the young king was a just master, the year was a good one for them both. Admetus saw much of his chief herdsman and came to respect him, while Apollo mightily increased the flocks of the king in return for his upright dealing. When the year came to an end, Admetus learned that not only was he a much richer man than before, but he had also acquired a powerful friend and protector. One of the first uses he made of Apollo's friendship was to gain himself a wife whom any prince in Greece would have been proud to marry.

Pelias, ruler of another Thessalian kingdom which he had seized by force from his cousin, had several daughters, but Alcestis was by far the loveliest. Not only was she beautiful, but she was skilled in all the arts of women. She was a notable spinner and maker of cloth, a good housewife, and performed everything with a charm which really came from a gentle, affectionate, and honorable nature. Even her dark and sinister father was fond of her and by no means anxious to let her marry and go to live in some other land. Nevertheless from the first moment she was old enough Pelias had been bothered by suitors for Alcestis. Every young man who saw her and a great many who only heard of her asked her father for her hand. At last Pelias became weary of the business and let it be known that he would marry his daughter only to the prince who could come to ask for her in a chariot drawn by a wild boar and a lion. Of course, no man could do this without help from the gods, so Pelias thought it most likely that he would be able to keep his daughter. But when Admetus accomplished the feat with Apollo's aid, Pelias at least could be satisfied that she was marrying a prosperous king who had the help of a powerful protector. He made the best of it, therefore, and the wedding was held with much rejoicing.

For several years after this Admetus was even happier than before. His parents thoroughly approved of his bride, who treated them with loving respect. Alcestis was a gentle, dignified queen, a beloved mistress of the household, and an affectionate mother. Towards her husband even though she had not chosen him herself, she showed all the love he could desire. Nothing seemed to be lacking. Admetus' face was radiant as he moved among his people; everything he did, he enjoyed. Men would mention him in conversation as an example of one who did not know what misfortune meant.

Meanwhile Apollo had not forgotten his friend, and loved to appear in human form from time to time and talk with him. But at last one day he came with a very grave face. "Admetus, my friend," he said seriously, "the Fates will spin out lasting happiness for no man. Each must have fortune and misfortune too, and so it is with you. It is decreed that in this very year your luck shall change. Within twelve months it is your fate to die."

The "fortunate" king went pale as ashes. His legs failed beneath him so that he sat down heavily, his hands limp at his sides. Then in a moment he leapt up and began to beg and implore Apollo. "You are powerful," he said desperately. "Save me from this. I am young, I am strong, no man enjoys life as I do. Why should I die? Life is full and rich for me; I enjoy every moment. Why, they say I even smile in sleep, and my dreams are glad ones. People point at me in the streets, 'There goes a happy man,' they say. And it is true. Why should I die when so many live who are weary of life, who are old, poor, sick, or lonely? Why should I die?"

"It is not possible to alter Fate," said Apollo gravely, "that is, not entirely. What I could do I have done. Someone, at least, must die, but I have won for you the promise that if another will die instead of you when the time comes, you may live." And with that hope the king was forced to be content.

From that time on nobody pointed to Admetus in the streets and called him the fortunate king. Indeed he made no secret of his misfortune, hoping always that someone who was tired of life would offer to change with him. But time went forward, and no one came. Other people who had envied his luck did not see why a less happy man should take on his load now that it was his turn to suffer. The year went on, and in all his kingdom no one offered the service that Admetus was too proud to ask. He found himself wandering past mean hovels, casting imploring glances at poor or crippled people. He fancied they understood what he wanted of them and that they looked at him mockingly. At last he could bear the city no longer and went out to manage his estate as he had been used. But the bleating of the countless lambs and the lowing of the cows in his great milking sheds only drove him to desperation. Finally his courage failed him, and as the long year came to an end, he went to see his father.

His father was outraged at the proposition Admetus put before him. "How dare you suggest such a thing?"

he shouted. "I have ten more good years of life and it is my own. I earned it and I shall enjoy it. Nobody ever called me the fortunate king. I toiled hard all my life for what I had. And now you, who have had everything given you and made no effort, want my last years of peace and happiness as well. What do you think a father is for, my son? Do you expect him always to give what you need? Oh no, I have given already and far too much. A father should receive—receive respect and affection and obedience from his children as the gods have ordained it. And this is all you offer: respect when it takes no trouble, affection when it is the easiest way. Get out of my sight."

"Selfish old man," answered Admetus, beside himself with fury at the direct refusal. "Now I know how much your only son is worth to you, not even a few miserable, toothless years of life."

"Get out of my sight," yelled the old man.

"I will," shouted Admetus, "and gladly, for you are no true parent of mine. At least I have a mother."

Admetus' mother was no more willing than her husband. "Look after yourself," she said indignantly. "You are not a baby any more. As long as you were one, I watched over you, fed you, dressed you, and sat up with you. You owe your life to me in any case. I never asked you as a baby to look after me. Now it is your turn."

"Now may you be cursed," retorted Admetus in a passion. "May the gods remember you as an unworthy mother, a hard, unfeeling woman. What use was it to give me life and nurse me up for this? A fine gift you gave! May you die unwept and unhonored."

"May Hera, the great queen mother, and Leto hear me," screamed the old woman. "They know what it is to have children. May they . . ." But Admetus turned away without hearing, for he felt that his time was come.

Admetus lay down on his couch and groaned aloud in bitter despair as he hid his face and waited for the coming of death. Meanwhile in her inner chamber the queen Alcestis quietly arose, kissed her two children, and gave them to her attendants. Then she bathed herself and put on fresh, white garments and went to the sacrifice. There she prayed the gods to take her life. Then as faintness came over her, she lay down on a couch and died quietly, while the groaning Admetus felt health surging back again and sat suddenly bolt upright. It was the miracle! His luck had saved him; he was not to die!

Even as he felt sure of this, he heard wails of women from the inner chamber and, rushing in, beheld the body of his wife. Admetus fell on his knees beside the corpse and kissed it, tears running down his cheeks. It had never occurred to him to ask Alcestis. He loved her, and she was so young. Everybody was so fond of her. She had as much to look forward to as he; there was no possible reason why she should die. Then as the greatness of the queen's sacrifice became clear to him, he saw for the first time how selfish he had been. Of course, he should shoulder his own misfortunes just like everybody else. What right had he running to his parents? He had had more luck than other people in any case. Why should it not be his turn? Admetus groaned again and would gladly have died if by so doing he could have brought his Alcestis to life, but it was too late.

An attendant touched him timidly on the shoulder. There was a stranger shouting for him in the great hall. It was Heracles, the mighty hero, returned from one of his deeds of strength and bursting to celebrate his achievement. He could not have come at a worse time, but he had to be met, so Admetus roused himself to go out and explain to him that this was a house of mourning. On the way, however, he thought better of it. Why should the happiness of Heracles be spoiled? Admetus had brought this sorrow on himself, and it was fitting he should bear it alone. He was utterly tired of his own selfishness. He stopped and gave orders to his servants to prepare a feast. He spoke firmly to them and they went obediently at last, muttering among themselves. Admetus went out to see his guest and made himself smile as he welcomed him.

The great, good-humored Heracles was not a sensitive man, and just now he was in an excited mood. He noticed nothing curious about Admetus or the servants; he was bent only on having a good time. And Admetus gave him a good time with wine, and song, and feasting. There was much laughter and a lot of noise. The disapproving servants, who had loved their mistress far more than they did Admetus, looked as gloomy as they dared. They grouped together in corners muttering, but for a

long time Heracles noticed nothing at all. When finally
the revelry was dying down and the excitement was
nearly over, Heracles perceived their disapproval and,
not liking it, called loudly for more wine. It was brought
to him, but with an air of reluctance which made him
strike his fist on the table and demand indignantly why
they could not serve him better. Admetus was out of the
room, and there was no one to restrain the anger of the
servants at what was going on. They told him exactly
what was the matter in the plainest terms.

Heracles was appalled at the trouble he had caused,
but he was also touched by Admetus. Never, he felt,
had he been entertained in so princely a fashion before.
It was like a great prince to put aside his grief and celebrate with a guest, even while his beloved wife lay dead
within his halls. Heracles questioned the servants as to
how long ago the queen had died, for he knew the way
to Hades well and he had a plan. He had been down to
Hades, and so great was his strength that not all the
monsters of that place had availed to keep him there.
He had bound the mighty Cerberus and brought him
up to earth alive. In fact, there was no feat that
Heracles was not equal to, for he was half divine and,
though he was a man now, he would be a god in time. It
might be possible to pursue Death and wrestle with him
for the spirit of Alcestis as they went hand in hand
down the steep path to the underworld. He said nothing to Admetus as yet and told the servants to keep
silence, but he took up his great club from the corner
where he had laid it, threw his lionskin over his shoul-

ders, and strode off in the direction of the dreadful path he had trodden once before.

It was early morning when Heracles came back, and with him walked a muffled figure. Admetus, summoned haggard and sleepless from his chamber, came, much tried but still courteous, to answer his guest's unreasonable demands. Heracles put back the cloak, and Alcestis looked at her husband as though she were just waking from sleep. As he ran forward and clasped her, he felt her come to life in his arms.

Alcestis and Admetus lived long after that time, happy yet generous to the poor and ailing. Admetus had learned both seriousness and sympathy. Though he was as prosperous as before, he had found that there were qualities more admirable than good luck, and he never cared again to be known by the title of "the fortunate king."

Pyramus and Thisbe

Pyramus and Thisbe were not Greeks, but lived in Babylon, which is an Asiatic city on the river Euphrates and much older than any of the cities of Greece. It was a rich and splendid place, whose hanging gardens were one of the seven wonders of the world. Being built on an open plain, it was made not of stone, but of baked bricks of river mud. Around it were immense brick fortifications, inside which narrow houses were huddled together.

Pyramus and Thisbe lived next door to each other and fell in love, but unfortunately their parents were extremely angry at this. The two were forbidden even to speak together, and since a father's command was absolute law in his household, it was a very serious matter to disobey. It happened, however, that the thin brick partition between the two houses was badly built. A brick was loose, and after a little trouble the lovers found that they could easily slip it out and in. At certain times of day when nobody was about, one of them would go up quietly and knock on the wall. Presently, if the other answered, they would take out the brick and whisper to each other very quietly through the hole.

It was a small, unsatisfactory opening, too narrow for even Thisbe's hand to pass right through. All they could do was to take turns at putting an ear to the wall, while both listened anxiously for the slightest sound of someone coming. Small wonder that they soon found things intolerable, and, as neither family showed the slightest sign of relenting, they determined to run away. In the city of Babylon they would soon have been found and taken back to their parents to be severely punished. They decided, therefore, to travel to some distant place where they could live without being asked too many questions.

The escape was carefully planned. They were to wait till night, when they would steal out unnoticed and each pass through a different gate of the city into the open country beyond. If they went together, the guards of the gate might notice and remember the pair, for few people went out of the town at night for fear of meeting robbers or wild beasts in the woods. Pyramus appointed a meeting place which he thought Thisbe could not fail to find, a monument called Ninus' Tomb not far outside the walls. It was a pleasant spot with a spring nearby and a tall mulberry tree hanging over it. In the shade of this tree Thisbe was to rest and wait for him.

Everything went well until Thisbe, who had passed through the nearest gate, arrived at Ninus' Tomb. She had never been out alone before, and all the little noises of the dark wood were terrifying to her. She had run the whole way from the gate, not daring to look around her, and now she sat down, drawing her cloak about her and trying to melt into the shadow of the mulberry tree.

There were rustlings in the dark thicket on the other side of the little clearing. Bushes seemed to move. Thisbe peered forward anxiously. There was a growling purr which could not have been the wind. She stiffened and held her breath to listen better. The bushes moved again; something very big was coming out of them. Thisbe saw a pair of gleaming eyes and the dark outline of a huge head. Now it was right out in the moonlight. It was a lioness.

Thisbe did not wait for the beast to get any nearer. She scrambled to her feet, dropped the entangling cloak, and ran for her life. She had no idea where she was going and only stopped when she tripped over a root and fell headlong. Then she did not dare get up, but lay trembling in some bushes against a bank, trying to still her breathing and to cower more closely to the ground.

The lioness had taken little notice of Thisbe. She had killed a calf already that night and was gorged with meat. Now she was slinking down to the spring to drink after her meal. On her way back to the thicket she noticed Thisbe's cloak. She sniffed at it distrustfully, bit at it with her bloodstained jaws, and played with it a little. Soon, however, she tired of the sport, and the black wood swallowed her up.

It was at this point that Pyramus arrived breathless

at Ninus' Tomb, his mind full of fears for Thisbe, of wild beasts, robbers, or even ghosts. Who could tell what she might meet alone in the dark wood? Pyramus drew his sword and carried it in his hand. All seemed still, however, and though he called Thisbe's name gently, nothing stirred beneath the tree. Then he saw the tracks of the lioness in the dust. Unspeakable fear came over him, and in another minute he had found the torn and bloody cloak and knew what must have happened. Thisbe had died horribly in some lion's jaws. It was all his fault. He had suggested Ninus' Tomb. He had planned that she should come to this dangerous place at night and alone. He could hardly bear to think of her dreadful fate, yet he could not help imagining it all the same. He would remember it for the rest of his life and know that it was all his fault. With that unendurable thought came a sudden resolution. Quickly he gripped his drawn sword low down on its blade and, holding it like a dagger, plunged it into his body with all his strength. He fell forward into the mulberry's shade, his head on the cloak, and his hand still clutching feebly at the sword.

In the meantime Thisbe's panic had died down a little, and she thought of Pyramus. What would become of him if he came to Ninus' Tomb and there met the lion? Whatever happened to her, she must go back. It was not easy to steal back quietly to the place where she had left a lion, and it took Thisbe a long time. At length, however, as the bright moon was getting low in the sky, she peered cautiously at the spot from a comparatively safe distance. There was a black shape lying in the shadow of the mulberry, the lion probably, but it was difficult to see. At that moment something moved. Thisbe caught her breath; it looked horribly like a hand. It moved again, and Thisbe running forward found the dying body of her lover before her feet. Without stopping to think how it all happened, she knelt, raised his head in her hands, kissed him, and called his name. The dying eyes opened slowly, the lips moved, but that was all.

Thisbe laid the head gently down and looked up, possessed by utter despair. She did not know why this had happened, but she was aware that her whole future was shattered. She could not go on without Pyramus, and she dared not return to her furious father. Her eye fell on the sword. What Pyramus could do, she could do. It was easy to plant the weapon point up in the loose, sandy soil. Thisbe shut her eyes and threw herself forward with all her strength.

Thus died the unfortunate lovers, but their fate was not forgotten. Their parents, reconciled by their love, buried them together in a common tomb. The gods changed the berries of the mulberry from silvery white to red, so that the tree which had watched over their deaths might be forever a reminder of their misfortune.

Baucis and Philemon

One time Zeus and Hermes came down to earth in human form and traveled through a certain district, asking for food and shelter as they went. For a long time they found nothing but refusals from both rich and poor until at last they came to a little, one-room cottage rudely thatched with reeds from the nearby marsh, where dwelled a poor old couple, Baucis and Philemon.

The two had little to offer, since they lived entirely from the produce of their plot of land and a few goats, fowl, and pigs. Nevertheless they were prompt to ask the strangers in and to set their best before them. The couch that they pulled forward for their guests was roughly put together from willow boughs, and the cushions on it were stuffed with straw. One table leg had to be propped up with a piece of broken pot, but Baucis scrubbed the top with fragrant mint and set some water on the fire. Meanwhile Philemon ran out into the garden to fetch a cabbage and then lifted down a piece of home-cured bacon from the blackened beam where it hung. While these were cooking, Baucis set out her best delicacies on the table. There were ripe olives, sour cherries pickled in wine, fresh onions and radishes, cream cheese, and eggs baked in the ashes of the fire. There was a big earthenware bowl in the midst of the table to mix their crude, homemade wine with water.

The second course had to be fruit, but there were nuts, figs, dried dates, plums, grapes, and apples, for this was their best season of the year. Philemon had even had it in mind to kill their only goose for dinner, and there was a great squawking and cackling that went on for a long time. Poor old Philemon wore himself out trying to catch that goose, but somehow the animal always got away from him until the guests bade him let it be, for they were well served as it was. It was a good meal, and the old couple kept pressing their guests to eat and drink, caring nothing that they were now consuming in one day what would ordinarily last them a week.

At last the wine sank low in the mixing bowl, and Philemon rose to fetch some more. But to his astonishment as he lifted the wineskin to pour, he found the bowl was full again as though it had not been touched at all. Then he knew the two strangers must be gods, and he and Baucis were awed and afraid. But the gods smiled kindly at them, and the younger, who seemed to do most of the talking, said, "Philemon, you have welcomed us beneath your roof this day when richer men refused us shelter. Be sure those shall be punished who would not help the wandering stranger, but you shall have whatever reward you choose. Tell us what you will have."

The old man thought for a little with his eyes bent on the ground, and then he said: "We have lived together here for many years, happy even though the times have been hard. But never yet did we see fit to turn a stranger from our gate or to seek a reward for entertaining him. To have spoken with the immortals face to face is a thing few men can boast of. In this small cottage, humble though it is, the gods have sat at meat. It is as unworthy of the honor as we are. If, therefore, you will do something for us, turn this cottage into a temple where the gods may always be served and where we may live out the remainder of our days in worship of them."

"You have spoken well," said Hermes, "and you shall have your wish. Yet is there not anything that you would desire for yourselves?"

Philemon thought again at this, stroking his straggly beard, and he glanced over at old Baucis with her thin, grey hair and her rough hands as she served at the table, her feet bare on the floor of trodden earth. "We have lived together for many years," he said again, "and in all that time there has never been a word of anger between us. Now, at last, we are growing old and our long companionship is coming to an end. It is the only thing that has helped us in the bad times and the source of our joy in the good. Grant us this one request, that when we come to die, we may perish in the same hour and neither of us be left without the other."

He looked at Baucis and she nodded in approval, so the old couple turned their eyes on the gods.

"It shall be as you desire," said Hermes. "Few men would have made such a good and moderate request."

Thereafter the house became a temple, and the neighbors, amazed at the change, came often to worship and left offerings for the support of the aged priest and priestess there. For many years Baucis and Philemon lived in peace, passing from old to extreme old age. At last, they were so old and bowed that it seemed they could only walk at all if they clutched one another. But still every evening they would shuffle a little way down the path that they might turn and look together at the beautiful little temple and praise the gods for the honor bestowed on them. One evening it took them longer than ever to reach the usual spot, and there they turned arm in arm to look back, thinking perhaps that it was the last time their limbs would support them so far. There as they stood, each one felt the other stiffen and change and only had time to turn and say once, "Farewell," before they disappeared. In their place stood two tall trees growing closely side by side with branches interlaced. They seemed to nod and whisper to each other in the passing breeze.

VI

ADVENTURE STORIES

Atalanta's Lovers

1. The Calydonian Hunt

Althaea, queen of Calydon, had borne a son to her husband, Oeneus, and amid scenes of great rejoicing the infant was named Meleager. Now on the seventh day as she lay in bed with her baby by her, Queen Althaea had a vision. It seemed to her that the wall of her chamber dissolved into a mist in which, far away, yet somehow near, she saw three old women spinning. They were incredibly yellow and ancient, yet their hands were quick and steady. One pulled fleecy wool from a distaff and twisted it into thread. Another drew out the end and began to wind it as it lengthened, while in the middle sat an old crone with a pair of open shears between which the thread passed as it was gathered in.

Althaea could see so clearly that she could even notice that the first who made the thread was quite unskillful. The thread ran thick here, and thin there almost to breaking, and between came knots and lumps such as would make it unfit for weaving. It seemed to her then that she had known all along that these were no ordinary women but the three Fates themselves, and that this was no weaving thread but the course of a man's life that they spun. Even as she knew this, she saw the yellow, skeleton-like head of the winder turn to the crouching spinner, and an old voice said: "Spin out the life of Meleager, sister; spin it out even and strong."

"How long?" said she with the shears, and the points quivered a little, "sisters; how long?"

"Not long," said she who was winding. "Cut when the log which burns on the queen's hearth is totally consumed to ash." And the pale blue eyes of all three turned slowly to the fire as the white thread ran between their fingers. The queen's eyes turned too. The great log on the hearth was burning merrily, already half consumed. Quick as a flash she looked back to the Fates, but the wall was solid again as though nothing had ever been there. Only an old voice seemed to say again, "Not long."

The queen leaped from her bed and with her naked hands snatched the burning wood from the fire. She beat it against the hearth; she smothered it in her robe. When it was dead and black, she fetched a pitcher of water and poured it over. At last she stood, hands black, clothes scorched, feet in a puddle of water, and looked at the ugly thing. She dared not leave it where her servants might find it and finish what was begun, so after some thought she wrapped it in a piece of costly embroidery and put it in a chest where her chief treasures were and of which she alone had the key. Thereafter the boy grew up strong and handsome, for the thread of his life as the Fates had foretold was even and strong.

When Meleager had reached manhood and was already famous for bravery, his father, Oeneus, brought great trouble on the land, for he neglected the worship of the goddess, Artemis, and she in anger sent to the woods of Calydon a monstrous boar. None had ever seen such an animal before. His bristles stood up along his spine like spikes of wood. His skin was tough as the rhinoceros. His great tusks were so enormous that only the elephant's could surpass them. The animal was as savage as he was formidable in appearance. Daily he trampled the growing corn and the green vineyards till the crops of the farmers were utterly ruined, and yet none could harm him. Dogs seemed helpless against him, spears glanced off his hide, and men who hunted him were crippled or killed.

At last Oeneus, in desperation, sent heralds all through Greece proclaiming a great hunt in the woods of Calydon and challenging every hero who wished for glory to try to slay the monstrous boar. From every kingdom all who were famous or who desired fame came to the meeting place. There was the fortunate Admetus with Jason, his cousin. There was Meleager himself with his two uncles, brothers of Althaea. There were many other heroes famous already or to be famous thereafter. Last of all there was Atalanta, the swift-running huntress, with her bow in hand and her ivory quiver on her shoulder.

As soon as Meleager saw Atalanta, he fell in love

with her beauty and her courage. He had eyes for no one else. This was by no means to the taste of other heroes who felt it was no part for a woman to join such a hunt with men. There were plenty there who disliked Atalanta and foremost among them were Meleager's two uncles. These took it upon themselves to advise the boy to pay her less attention and were still further enraged when they were disregarded.

Nothing, however, came of the matter openly, and when the hunt began, Atalanta was included with no more than a secret muttering among the men. The boar's lair was in a dense wood, thick with underbrush, which none had dared to enter since he came. Around most of this the men stretched their strongest hunting nets. Then they took stations all about, while some went down the trail with packs of dogs to rout the monster out.

When the boar rushed out, all was confusion. The animal scattered the yelping dogs and made straight for the men. The hunters were many, but they were not all together in one place. Nor could they aim their spears in time, for the boar's speed was too great. Besides, they were fighting in dense woodland where it was very hard to move about and where spears glanced off branches without even hitting the raging beast. He, on the other hand, charged straight through the thicket and laid two heroes low. Two more were knocked down and trampled, while a third saved himself only by vaulting hastily into a tree, using his spear as a pole. Rocks and arrows were whizzing around the beast, but nothing hit except the blunt shaft of one spear. This slowed his rush. The yelping dogs closed in on him, and while they did him no harm, they did bring him for a moment to bay. He stopped and glared at them, red-eyed and snorting. In that moment an arrow from Atalanta's bow grazed along his back and stuck below the ear. The animal was only slightly hurt, but he turned and made off in the direction from which he had come, while Meleager raised a joyful shout that Atalanta had drawn first blood and then headed the rush down the trail. There was a desperate struggle when the boar was brought to bay again, but at last he fell, and the spear that gave the final stroke was Meleager's.

There was great rejoicing as the heroes gathered round to marvel at the great beast and measure his mighty tusks. Meleager was the hero of the hour, perhaps the more because he was the host and because the heroes did not wish to remember that the timely arrow which wounded the boar and turned him at a critical moment was Atalanta's. Meleager sensed this feeling and, drunk with his achievement, could not conceal his resentment from his older companions. He received, therefore, the spoils of the chase, the head and skin of the fearsome monster, which were presented to him with great ceremony, and then offered them to Atalanta, saying that the first wound and the chief credit were hers.

At this insulting treatment of the honor paid to him, there was a tense silence, broken after a moment by Althaea's two brothers. As Meleager's uncles, these saw fit to reprove him for his behavior in awarding the prize against the wishes of the other heroes. Meleager was far from quietly putting up with this. One retort led to another, and the furious uncles told him exactly what they thought of Atalanta, her forward manners and un-womanly behavior. This was too much for the excited lover. In a blind passion he threw his spear at one of the speakers with all his might and killed him instantly. Before he had time to realize what he had done, the other fell on him and in self-defense he struck again, killing him likewise.

It had all happened too quickly for anyone to inter-fere. Afterwards there was muttering and great dismay. Meleager himself was appalled but covered his feelings with sullen defiance. So the group broke up, most of them ranging themselves in a procession around the biers of the dead, but Meleager still stayed with Ata-lanta and declared loudly that his uncles had brought death on themselves.

Althaea was like a madwoman when the message came. She cared little for her husband; her pride was in her brothers and her son. All the reports announced that Meleager had struck first, had started the quarrel by his open preference of Atalanta. Althaea too felt that ranging the woods with heroes was no occupation for a woman. Meleager was in the wrong from first to last— not only had he forgotten the great respect which younger men should always pay to elder, not only had he slain his own kinsmen, the greatest crime a man could commit, but he showed no sign of shame or sorrow. Althaea would speak to no one and eat nothing. She went to her room and paced up and down there all night and all day. At last as the evening came, the frightened servants in the doorway heard the queen speak. "I am cold," she said to them between her teeth. "Light me a fire."

When they came back with materials, the chest by the far wall was open and the queen held in her hands a blackened piece of wood. "Let justice be done," she said to herself and put it in the flame. Then she drew up a chair and sat down to watch it burn.

Even at that moment on his way home from the woods of Calydon, Meleager gasped, clutched himself and fell writhing to the earth. "I am burning up," was all he could say, and he died in agony, no drink or cool application being capable of relieving his pain. But the queen far away in her chamber, as she saw the last piece crumble into ash, lifted her hand from her side before her women could stop her and drove a dagger through her heart. So ended the Calydonian hunt amid mourning and lamentation. Each of the heroes returned soberly to his home, and Atalanta, saying no word to any, went back to the woods from whence she came.

2. The Winning of Atalanta

Atalanta hunted in the wild woods as she used to do. No one could tell whether she sorrowed for Meleager, for she said no word of that, but though many young men came to woo her, she steadfastly refused to marry.

She loved her wild freedom, so she said, and had no desire to be mistress of a household or mother of children. Every suitor she counted as an enemy. Her father was not of the same mind, however, and for a long time he vainly urged his daughter to marry. At last, losing his patience, he insisted she make a choice among her suitors. Atalanta could not refuse her father directly, but she decided to outwit him if she could. She therefore set up a racecourse in a grassy valley, and declared that any who wished to marry must first race with her. He who could outrun her should be her husband, but if she were the faster, the beaten man should die. By this means she hoped to avoid having any suitors at all, while yet if they did persist, she could rely on her speed to defeat them.

At first the challenge of Atalanta only acted as a stimulus to her suitors. There were plenty of young men ready to risk their lives for fame and for the winning of so beautiful a bride. Perhaps they hoped that she would not be so cruel as to carry out her threat. But after a time when it was known that the swift and slender Atalanta ran like the very wind itself and that she always demanded the penalty of death when she was the winner, fewer and fewer men came to race with her. Spectators thronged the racecourse instead, drawn to see so desperate a struggle and to catch sight of so cruel a maiden. Among these there was small pity for the unfortunate suitors. People thought they were fools to challenge the girl when many other beautiful and far kinder maidens might be won.

Among these spectators came Hippomenes, despising in his heart both the men who ran in the contest and the worthless girl who caused death to so many. So he thought until he saw her running, swift as a wild deer, hair fluttering behind her and breath coming easily between her parted lips. Behind her toiled another runner, laboring with all his strength, but Atalanta spared no glance for him. Even when he was led away, she only stood there, cheeks flushed and panting slightly, looking out on the wild wood which was her home.

Hippomenes had never seen anyone so beautiful. This was indeed a woman to die for, yet die he very likely would if he raced with her, for he had watched her running and seen that she did not put forth all her strength. Yet he made the challenge, and when the girl came — as was her custom — and said a few words to discourage him from running, he thought she looked on him kindly and that the color came into her cheeks as she met his eyes. But for all these signs of favor, he knew she would not spare him. He went then to the temple of Aphrodite and prayed earnestly for her aid. The goddess of love and beauty had no sympathy for Atalanta, worshiper of the cold moon goddess, Artemis. She came, therefore, to Hippomenes when he called her, put something into his hand, and gave him counsel. With this Hippomenes waited in confidence for the morning.

When the race began, Hippomenes shot a little ahead of Atalanta and made a great show of putting out all his strength. But soon he seemed to fail a little, and swift feet came up behind him. Then for a moment the two raced side by side. The girl glanced at her rival uneasily, and Hippomenes saw with joy that she was reluctant to pass him. Yet he knew that soon she would, and he stumbled a little and seemed to fail, in order that she needs must draw ahead. Then he smiled to himself as he watched her. She was easy and confident. She thought he was beaten and that she could play with him. At that he drew forth one of the things that the goddess had given him and threw it before Atalanta on the path. It was a golden apple, a miracle of a fruit which the goddess had plucked herself from a living tree. It rolled along in front of Atalanta, and the wonderful beauty of it tempted her. She must have it, and the man was failing; there was plenty of time. She stooped to pick it up, and in that minute Hippomenes passed her. Still he seemed to be laboring and failing, though actually he ran fast. Atalanta marveled that with the efforts he made his speed did not slacken, and she was sure that soon it must. Again she ran evenly after him, caught him and passed him, though she did not wish to. Again a golden apple rolled before her on the path.

Atalanta was angry at the challenge of this second apple. She knew now that the man, poor runner as he was, intended to win by trickery. She would accept his challenge and win all the same. His hoarse breath seemed louder and louder, and greater the effort with which he ran. Nevertheless as she picked up the second apple, he passed her again. Now Atalanta was angry with him and ran after him, swifter than the wild deer, like the woodland wind itself. She passed him like the flickering shadow of a leaf. The goal was now in sight, and for the last time Hippomenes threw a golden apple. Then as the maiden stooped for it, he cast all pretences to the winds and ran for his very life. Quick as a flash Atalanta was after him, yet the goal was very near. If she had known that he was not really exhausted, she would never have dared to stoop for the third apple. One moment she was two paces behind, and the next her breath, panting now, seemed almost in his hair. But the winning post was only a few yards ahead, and still the girl was half a pace behind. They seemed for a breathless second to race side by side, and then with a final effort Hippomenes touched the winning post an instant before Atalanta's outstretched hand.

Such was the winning of Atalanta, and the story says that the bride in spite of her anger at being tricked was not unhappy to be won. At all events, Hippomenes married her amid great rejoicing, thanks to Aphrodite, who had known that a woman would certainly be tempted by the gift of the three golden apples.

The Killing of the Chimera

The bravest and most handsome among the princes of Argos who acknowledged King Proitos as their overlord was the young Bellerophon. Even Anteia, Proitos' wife, fell in love with him. When she saw, however, that the young man cared nothing for her, she wanted revenge and accused Bellerophon to her husband, saying that he was making love to her. King Proitos, who believed his wife completely, swore that Bellerophon should pay with his life for the treason. Since, however, he had no proof but his wife's word, the king was unwilling to accuse the young man openly, nor, powerful as he was, did he dare to put to death a popular young hero without giving some reason. Deciding, therefore, to have his revenge by craft, he gave Bellerophon a sealed letter to Anteia's father, Iobates, asking his father-in-law to put the messenger to death.

When Iobates, king of Lycia, received Proitos' message, he was in despair. He had taken an immediate liking to the handsome and courageous Bellerophon and had entertained him royally for ten days without even asking to see the letter he carried. In those days men would make much of a messenger so that he might feel welcome for his own sake, not only because of what he brought. Iobates could not believe the accusation. He knew his daughter for a jealous, crafty woman, and he judged Bellerophon to be honorable. Besides, the young man had been introduced to his whole court and had received open marks of favor. It was hardly possible to murder him now, yet to let him go was to cause an open quarrel with Proitos. Iobates pondered long over his problem until at last he resolved, as Proitos had, to get his way by cunning.

That evening when the courtiers sat feasting in the palace and the minstrel arose to sing, Iobates bade him tell the tale of Phaethon, who tried to equal the immortals by driving the chariot of the sun. Then as the minstrel's tale came to an end, and Phaethon fell from heaven in a trail of gleaming fire, the king turned to his chief guest and drank a toast to him, saying, "Tell me, Bellerophon, do you not think that Phaethon was wise? He aspired to be like a god, and though he failed, his end was glorious, and he has become a hero of song. Would you not rather try some impossible feat and die than rest content with the knowledge that there were things you dared not do?"

"I dare do all things," answered the young Bellerophon, his blue eyes sparkling. "I dare even mount to Olympus and battle with the gods. What matter if I fail? I shall still die a hero because I aimed for mighty deeds."

"Then do a deed for me," Iobates leaned forward quickly. "Rid me of the monster that no man in my kingdom dares to face. Kill me the Chimera."

"Gladly," said the eager Bellerophon, and he drank deep to his host, for he had already heard of this monster and thought that the killing of it would be a glorious adventure. The Chimera was a nightmare of a creature with three heads, a lion's, a goat's, and a dragon's. Its body also had three parts. The forequarters were those of a lion, the hindquarters those of a goat, and it had the long, scaly tail of a dragon. Out of the dragon mouth came raging fire, so that for miles around its lair the land was desolate, and the farms lay blackened and deserted.

As Bellerophon said goodnight to his host, both men were well pleased. To Iobates it seemed most likely that the Chimera would kill Bellerophon and accomplish the desire of King Proitos. If not, however, at least the kingdom of Lycia would be rid of the dreadful beast. Bellerophon on his side was glad at the thought of the great adventure. In his mind was already a plan by which he might approach the monster. He hoped to capture first the horse, Pegasus, and with his aid to conquer the Chimera.

Pegasus was a great, white, winged horse, so beautiful that it was a pleasure to watch him move, but he was very fierce and allowed no one to bridle him. Daily he could be seen racing the plains, gleaming, red-eyed, and savage. From a safe distance men could watch him wheel and gallop, mane and tail streaming in the wind, or spread great wings and soar up into the distant blue.

When he came down to his favorite stream to drink, however, he might be approached, and many had come there and struggled in vain to master him.

Along the banks of this river came Bellerophon in the grey early morning, having in his hand a golden bridle which the goddess Athene had given him. When he came to the spot where the stems were trampled and great hoof marks showed in the mud, he crept into a nearby thicket and lay closely hidden. Soon, as the goddess Aurora opened wide the doors for the chariot of the sun, there was a thudding of hooves, and Bellerophon, peering out, saw the great horse racing the plain.

Pegasus seemed frantic with joy. He flung himself from side to side, reared back his great head, and pawed the air. Then he was off, racing up and down the green meadow, leaping the low bushes, and snorting with delight. All the while his white wings stood up from his shoulders like a feathery cloud, and the sun made silver ripples on his sides. Never was there such a horse. In the blazing noon he leapt into the air and sped straight up like an arrow, seeming to dart at the fiery sun. When he came back, it was afternoon, and he glided in from the west along the slanting sunbeams, alighting as gently as a little breath of wind. Now he walked slowly across the flowering meadow, paused at the bank to look over the thicket, and seeing no danger, bent his head to drink. Quietly Bellerophon parted the bushes, crept down the bank, and cast Athene's bridle around the horse's head.

Pegasus reared with a sudden movement, and the hero, still holding the bridle, stumbled and fell head-long. Then the horse felt the tug of Athene's magic, and instead of dashing the bold mortal to pieces with his hooves, he dropped back, so that Bellerophon, leaping to his feet, could vault onto the mighty back. Pegasus felt the weight and bounded into the air, but as he did so, the hero knew with a thrill of excitement that he was the horse's master. The leaps and dives and wheels were signs of joy, not anger. The horse responded to the slightest pressure of his knee. Indeed, the hero in his gleaming bronze seemed made for the glorious steed; the two appeared to be a single creature. Wind whistled in the yellow curls of Bellerophon and in the horsehair crest of his helmet. The white cloak streamed from his shoulders as he rode. Both gleamed like the immortals as they sped across the sky, the horse silver as a moonlit cloud, the man in his bronze armor blazing like the sun itself.

Together they soared over the plains of Lycia, while the sun still lingered in the sky, pouring its golden light on the rich farms, the green corn, and the red herds of cattle. Lycia lay smiling and prosperous beneath their feet, save that around the Chimera's lair all was black and deserted. Farmhouses were roofless shells sur-rounded by burned stumps of trees.

The monster was sprawled across a pile of rocks, its three heads restlessly scanning the horizon and its long grey tail coiled between the stones. As the horse and rider flashed across the sky, Bellerophon fitted an ar-

row to his bow. The monster saw them come and reared
itself on its giant forepaws, while from the dragon
mouth went up a roaring burst of flames until all the air
around it quivered from the heat. Bellerophon let fly his
arrow, and it sank deep into the monster's hide. Then
the Chimera roared again and gathering itself together
reared up on its hind legs. Pegasus darted down
through the raging flame far swifter than a falling stone,
while Bellerophon, spear in hand, stabbed blindly
through the smoke. He felt the claws thud against his
shield, saw the huge lion head snarling almost in his
face. Then they had sped through the fire and beyond,
and Pegasus was wheeling for another swoop.

Bellerophon gripped his spear and once more felt
the air whistle past him as they dived and met the hot
breath of the Chimera. Once more he lunged with all
his strength and missed. Half-blinded he saw the deadly
goat's horns make an upward slash far too swiftly for
him to lower the protecting shield. In an instant they
would have ripped him, but Pegasus turned quickly
and was out of the flame in the pure, cool air above.

Bellerophon reeled in his saddle and breathed in
gasps. Swift though the horse had been, the hero's arms
were scorched as he leaned forward to drive his spear
straight at the deadly thing. A third time they dropped.
Again Bellerophon peered with reddened eyes at the
half-seen monster. Straight for the open dragon mouth
they swooped, and Bellerophon with a mighty effort
gripped his spear and drove it with all his force into the
fiery throat. Fire boiled around him and played up his

arms, but he clutched the tighter in his agony and pressed the spear point home. The wooden shaft of the spear blackened, smoked, and burst into flame, yet still he held it in bare hands and pushed down with all his might until at last the horse wheeled upward and the spear was wrenched from his grasp. Bellerophon fell forward on the neck of Pegasus, for he could grasp nothing with his black and swollen hands. Beneath him on the ground the monster lay dying, its fiery breath drowned in a welter of hissing blood, and the stump end of the spear shaft still protruding from its throat.

Great was the rejoicing in Lycia at the death of the horrible beast, and great was the concern of King Iobates. The problem of how to kill such a hero was now more difficult than ever.

Iobates sent him against his enemies, the Solymi. Bellerophon killed them and returned. Then he was sent to fight the fierce warrior women, the Amazons. Still he came back victorious. Finally Iobates even set men in ambush to kill the hero as he came home. Bellerophon fell on them and slew them, taking them for common robbers and leaving not one of them alive.

Every time the hero returned in glory, King Iobates had to make much of him. He was always having to feast him, and all the time he liked him more and more. Finally when he saw how much his people loved Bellerophon, how invincible he was, how handsome, and how noble, he determined to forget Proitos' instructions and to keep Bellerophon for his friend. Accordingly he offered him one of his daughters in marriage and made him the heir to the kingdom.

Bellerophon married the Lycian princess, in time became king of that land, and had sons who were mighty heroes. His final end was as glorious as his life, for he mounted the winged horse, Pegasus, and flew up into the heavens, determined to reach Olympus or die in the attempt. The gods, however, do not allow the rivalry of mortals. Zeus cast him down from the horse with a thunderbolt, and he fell, like Phaethon, in a trail of gleaming fire. Pegasus flew on alone and came to the stables of Zeus, where he became the horse of the Muses and lives forever, feeding on the nectar of the gods.

Medusa's Head

King Acrisios of Argos was a hard, selfish man. He hated his brother, Proitos, who later drove him from his kingdom and he cared nothing for his daughter, Danae. His whole heart was set on having a son who should succeed him, but since many years went by and still he had only the one daughter, he sent a message to the oracle of Apollo to ask whether he should have more children of his own. The answer of the oracle was terrible. Acrisios should have no son, but his daughter, Danae, would bear him a grandchild who should grow up to kill him. At these words Acrisios was beside himself with fear and rage. Swearing that Danae should never have a child to murder him, he had a room built underground and lined all through with brass. Thither he conducted Danae and shut her up, bidding her spend the rest of her life alone.

It is possible to thwart the plans of mortal men, but never those of the gods. Zeus himself looked with pity at the unfortunate girl, and it is said he descended to her through the tiny hole that gave light and air to her chamber, pouring himself down into her lap in the form of a shower of gold.

When word came to the king from those who brought food and drink to his daughter that the girl was with child, Acrisios was angry and afraid. He would have liked best to murder both Danae and her infant son, but he did not dare for fear of the gods' anger at so hideous a crime. He made, therefore, a great chest of wood with bands of brass about it. Shutting up the girl and her baby inside, he cast them into the sea, thinking that they would either drown or starve.

Again the gods came to the help of Danae, for they caused the planks of the chest to swell until they fitted tightly and let no water in.

The chest floated for some days and was cast up at last on an island. There Dictys, a fisherman, found it and took Danae to his brother, Polydectes, who was king of the island. Danae was made a servant in the palace, yet before many years had passed, both Dictys and Polydectes had fallen in love with the silent, golden-haired girl. She in her heart preferred Dictys, yet since his brother was king, she did not dare to make her choice. Therefore she hung always over Perseus, pretending that mother love left her no room for any other, and year after year a silent frown would cross Polydectes' face as he saw her caress the child.

At last, Perseus became a young man, handsome and strong beyond the common and a leader among the youths of the island, though he was but the son of a poor servant. Then it seemed to Polydectes that if he could once get rid of Perseus, he could force Danae to become his wife, whether she would or not. Meanwhile, in order to lull the young man's suspicions, he pretended that he intended to marry a certain noble maiden and would collect a wedding gift for her. Now the custom was that this gift of the bridegroom to the bride was in part his own and in part put together from the marriage presents of his friends and relatives. All the young men, therefore, brought Polydectes a present, excepting Perseus, who was his servant's son and possessed nothing to bring. Then Polydectes said to the others, "This young man owes me more than any of you, since I took him in and brought him up in my own house, and yet he gives me nothing."

Perseus answered in anger at the injustice of the charge, "I have nothing of my own, Polydectes, yet ask me what you will, and I will fetch it, for I owe you my life."

At this Polydectes smiled, for it was what he had intended, and he answered, "Fetch me, if this is your boast, the Gorgon's head."

Now the Gorgons, who lived far off on the shores of the ocean, were three fearful sisters with hands of brass, wings of gold, and scales like a serpent. Two of them had scaly heads and tusks like the wild boar, but the third, Medusa, had the face of a beautiful woman with hair of writhing serpents, and so terrible was her expression that all who looked on it were immediately turned to stone. This much Perseus knew of the Gorgons, but of how to find or kill them, he had no idea. Nevertheless he had given his promise, and though he saw now the satisfaction of King Polydectes, he was bound to keep his word. In his perplexity he prayed to the wise goddess, Athene, who came to him in a vision and promised him her aid.

"First, you must go," she said, "to the sister Phorcides, who will tell you the way to the nymphs who guard the hat of darkness, the winged sandals, and the knapsack which can hold the Gorgon's head. Then I will give you a shield and my brother, Hermes, a sword which shall be made of adamant, the hardest rock. For nothing else can kill the Gorgon, since so venomous is her blood that a mortal sword when plunged in it is eaten away. But when you come to the Gorgons, invisible in your hat of darkness, turn your eyes away from them and look only on their reflection in your gleaming shield. Thus you may kill the monster without yourself being turned to stone. Pass her sisters by, for they are immortal, but smite off the head of Medusa with the hair of writhing snakes. Then put it in your knapsack and return, and I will be with you."

The vision ended, and with the aid of Athene, Perseus set out on the long journey to seek the Phorcides. These live in a dim cavern in the far north, where nights and days are one and where the whole earth is overspread with perpetual twilight. There sat the three old women mumbling to one another, crouched in a dim heap together, for they had but one eye and one tooth between them which they passed from hand to hand.

Perseus came quietly behind them, and as they fumbled for the eye, he put his strong, brown hand next to one of the long, yellow ones, so that the old crone thought that it was her sister's and put the eye in it. There was a high scream of anger when they discovered the theft, and much clawing and groping in the dim recesses of the cavern. But they were helpless in their blindness and Perseus could laugh at them. At length for the price of their eye they told him how to reach the nymphs, and Perseus, laying the eye quickly in the hand of the nearest sister, fled as fast as he could before she could use it.

Again it was a far journey to the garden of the nymphs, where it is always sunshine and the trees bear golden apples. But the nymphs are friends of the wise gods and hate the monsters of darkness and the spirits of anger and despair. Therefore, they received Perseus with rejoicing and put the hat of darkness on his head, while on his feet they bound the golden, winged sandals, which are those Hermes wears when he runs down the slanting sunbeams or races along the pathways of the wind. Next, Perseus put on his back the silver sack with the gleaming tassels of gold and flung across his shoulder the black-sheathed sword that was the gift of Hermes. On his left arm he fitted the shield that Athene gave, a gleaming silver shield like a mirror, plain without any marking. Then he sprang into the air and ran, invisible like the rushing wind, far out over the white-capped sea, across the yellow sands of the eastern desert, over strange streams and towering mountains,

until at last he came to the shores of the distant ocean
which flowed round all the world.

There was a grey gorge of stone by the ocean's edge,
where lay Medusa and her sisters sleeping in the dim
depths of the rock. All up and down the cleft the stones
took fantastic shapes of trees, beasts, birds, or serpents.
Here and there a man who had looked on the terrible
Medusa stood forever with horror on his face. Far over
the twilit gorge Perseus hovered invisible, while he
loosened the pale, strange sword from its black sheath.
Then with his face turned away and eyes on the silver
shield he dropped, slow and silent as a falling leaf,
down through the rocky cleft, twisting and turning past
countless strange grey shapes, down from the bright
sunlight into a chill, dim shadow echoing and re-echo-
ing with the dashing of waves on the tumbled rocks
beneath. There on the heaped stones lay the Gorgons
sleeping together in the dimness, and even as he looked
on them in the shield, Perseus felt stiff with horror at
the sight.

Two of the Gorgons lay sprawled together, shaped
like women yet scaled from head to foot as serpents are.
Instead of hands they had gleaming claws like eagles,
and their feet were dragons' feet. Skinny metallic wings
like bats' wings hung from their shoulders. Their faces
were neither snake nor woman, but part both, like faces
in a nightmare. These two lay arm in arm and never
stirred. Only the blue snakes still hissed and writhed
round the pale, set face of Medusa, as though even in

sleep she were troubled by an evil dream. She lay by herself, arms outstretched, face upwards, more beautiful and terrible than living man may bear. All the crimes and madnesses of the world rushed into Perseus' mind as he gazed at her image in the shield. Horror stiffened his arm as he hovered over her with his sword uplifted. Then he shut his eyes to the vision and in the darkness struck.

There was a great cry and a hissing. Perseus groped for the head and seized it by the limp and snaky hair. Somehow he put it in his knapsack and was up and off, for at the dreadful scream the sister Gorgons had awakened. Now they were after him, their sharp claws grating against his silver shield. Perseus strained forward on the pathway of the wind like a runner, and behind him the two sisters came, smelling out the prey they could not see. Snakes darted from their girdles, foam flew from their tusks, and the great wings beat the air. Yet the winged sandals were even swifter than they, and Perseus fled like the hunted deer with the speed of desperation. Presently the horrible noise grew faint behind him, the hissing of snakes and the sound of the bat wings died away. At last the Gorgons could smell him no longer and returned home unavenged.

By now Perseus was over the Lybian desert, and as the blood from the horrible head touched the sand, it changed to serpents, from which the snakes of Africa are descended.

The storms of the Lybian desert blew against Perseus in clouds of eddying sand, until not even the di-

vine sandals could hold him on his course. Far out to
sea he was blown, and then north. Finally, whirled
around the heavens like a cloud of mist, he alighted in
the distant west where the giant, Atlas, held up on his
shoulders the heavens from the earth. There the weary
giant, crushed under the load of centuries, begged
Perseus to show him Medusa's head. Perseus uncovered for him the dreadful thing, and Atlas was changed
to the mighty mountain whose rocks rear up to reach
the sky near the gateway to the Atlantic. Perseus himself, returning eastwards and still battling with the
wind, was driven south to the land of Ethiopia, where
king Cepheus reigned with his wife, Cassiopeia.

As Perseus came wheeling in like a gull from the
ocean, he saw a strange sight. Far out to sea the water
was troubled, seething and boiling as though stirred by
a great force moving in its depths. Huge, sullen waves
were starting far out and washing inland over sunken
trees and flooded houses. Many miles of land were under water, and as he sped over them, he saw the muddy
sea lapping around the foot of a black, upstanding rock.
Here on a ledge above the water's edge stood a young
girl chained by the arms, lips parted, eyes open and
staring, face white as her linen garment. She might
have been a statue, so still she stood, while the light
breeze fluttered her dress and stirred her loosened hair.
As Perseus looked at her and looked at the sea, the water began to boil again, and miles out a long, grey scaly
back of vast length lifted itself above the flood. At that
there was a shriek from a distant knoll where he could

dimly see the forms of people, but the girl shrank a little and said nothing. Then Perseus, taking off the hat of darkness, alighted near the maiden to talk to her, and she, though nearly mad with terror, found words at last to tell him her tale.

Her name was Andromeda, and she was the only child of the king and of his wife, Cassiopeia. Queen Cassiopeia was exceedingly beautiful, so that all people marveled at her. She herself was proud of her dark eyes, her white, slender fingers, and her long black hair, so proud that she had been heard to boast that she was fairer even than the sea nymphs who are daughters of Nereus. At this Nereus in wrath stirred up Poseidon, who came flooding in over the land, covering it far and wide. Not content with this he sent a vast monster from the dark depths of the bottomless sea to ravage the whole coast of Ethiopia. When the unfortunate king and queen had sought the advice of the oracle on how to appease the god, they had been ordered to sacrifice their only daughter to the sea monster Poseidon had sent. Not daring for their people's sake to disobey, they had chained her to this rock, where she now awaited the beast who should devour her.

Perseus comforted Andromeda as he stood by her on the rock, and she shrank closer against him while the great, grey back writhed its half-mile length slowly towards the land. Then bidding Andromeda hide her face, Perseus sprang once more into the air, unveiling the dreadful head of dead Medusa to the monster which reared its dripping jaws yards high into the air. The

mighty tail stiffened all of a sudden, the boiling of the water ceased, and only the gentle waves of the receding ocean lapped around a long, grey ridge of stone. Then Perseus freed Andromeda and restored her to her father and beautiful mother. Thereafter with their consent he married her amid scenes of tremendous rejoicing, and with his bride set sail at last for the kingdom of Polydectes.

Polydectes had lost no time on the departure of Perseus. First he had begged Danae to become his wife, and then he had threatened her. Undoubtedly he would have got his way by force if Danae had not fled in terror to Dictys. The two took refuge at the altar of a temple whence Polydectes did not dare drag them away. So matters stood when Perseus returned. Polydectes was enraged to see him, for he had hoped at least that Danae's most powerful protector would never return. But now, seeing him famous and with a king's daughter to wife, he could not contain himself. Openly he laughed at the tale of Perseus, saying that the hero had never killed the Gorgon, only pretended to, and that now he was claiming an honor he did not deserve. At this Perseus, enraged by the insult and by reports of his mother's persecution, said to him, "You asked me for the Gorgon's head. Behold it!" And with that he lifted it high, and Polydectes became stone.

Then Perseus left Dictys to be king of that island, but he himself went back to the Grecian mainland to seek out his grandfather, Acrisios, who was once again king of Argos. First, however, he gave back to the gods

the gifts they had given him. Hermes took back the
golden sandals and the hat of darkness, for both are his.
But Athene took Medusa's head, and she hung it on a
fleece around her neck as part of her battle equipment,
where it may be seen in statues and portraits of the
warlike goddess.

Perseus took ship for Greece, but his fame had gone
before him, and king Acrisios fled secretly from Argos
in terror, since he remembered the prophecy and feared
that Perseus had come to avenge the wrongs of Danae.
The trembling old Acrisios took refuge in Larissa,
where it happened the king was holding a great athletic
contest in honor of his dead father.

Heroes from all over Greece, among whom was
Perseus, came to the games. As Perseus was competing
at the discus throwing, he threw high into the air and
far beyond the rest. A strong wind caught the discus as
it spun so that it left the course marked out for it and
was carried into the stands. People scrambled away to
right and left. Only Acrisios was not nimble enough.
The heavy weight fell full on his foot and crushed his
toes, and at that the feeble old man, already weakened
by his terrors, died from the shock. Thus the prophecy
of Apollo was fulfilled at last; Acrisios was killed by his
grandson. Then Perseus came into his kingdom, where
he reigned with Andromeda long and happily.

The Golden Fleece

1. The Challenge

Cretheus, founder of Iolcos, lived long as king of that little town and died in prosperity, leaving three sons who might have succeeded him. Nevertheless, his great-nephew, the dark, intriguing Pelias, persuaded the townsfolk to put him on the throne. Cretheus' two younger sons were driven out and became in time rulers of neighboring cities, one of them being the father of Admetus. The eldest son, Aeson, the true heir to his father's throne, Pelias did not care to let out of his sight. To kill him would have been useless, since one of his brothers would have inherited his claim. Pelias merely guarded him carefully, allowed him sufficient wealth, but forced him to live in obscurity. In spite of this he determined to get rid of Aeson's baby son. Young men grow up to be ambitious; it was better to put the child to death. He sent messengers to seize the baby, but was enraged to find that they had come too late. Aeson had sent a servant out secretly to take the child far away into the mountains where King Pelias could never come. There the boy was delivered to the wise centaur, Cheiron, half horse, half man, to be brought up in the woodlands and to learn all the things that a hero should. Meanwhile King Pelias, dismayed by his failure to remove this one threat, sent to ask the oracle what his chances were of remaining safe on his throne.

"Beware," said the voice of the oracle, "the man who comes limping into the marketplace with one sandal and one foot bare." With that warning Pelias had to be content.

Long years went by during which the people of Iolcos learned to respect their tyrant, but loved him little. Pelias was a jealous man, quick to seize the least breath of suspicion. He was a cruel king, and yet he had known how to keep Iolcos at peace and make it powerful, cementing alliances with nearby princes through the marriages of his daughters.

All this while in the depths of the woodland, Aeson's son was growing up. The boy was called Jason; in appearance he was blue-eyed and golden-haired, the very picture of a hero. Cheiron was tutor to a whole group of noble boys, among whom Jason learned everything that a prince should know. Much of his training was in riding, jumping, wrestling, and mastery of the weapons of war, but Cheiron also taught him to play the lyre, to sing, to make poetry, and to recite by heart long stories of the deeds of heroes which the minstrels of old had made.

Among the boys with Cheiron, Jason was a leader and a favorite, for he was open-hearted and daring, ever quick to take a chance, good-humored and easy-going. Cheiron himself was proud of the boy, yet at times he looked at him rather thoughtfully. He was brave, but he was not cunning. People liked him, but he took advantage of this a little too easily. Therefore at last when the time came for Jason to go and claim his inheritance from King Pelias, Cheiron was unwilling to part with him.

"Be careful of King Pelias," was his final word, "for he is both hard and clever. Do not trust him, or he will trap you." But Jason said good-bye with confidence, paying little attention.

It was a long road from the wood of Cheiron to the city of Iolcos, and on the way Jason lost a sandal as he carried a poor old woman across a flooded river. The old woman was Hera in disguise, and when she saw he was good-natured and kindly, she appeared in her true shape to him and blessed him, promising to be with him always. Limping in his one sandal, Jason came quite openly into the marketplace of Iolcos and began to question the folk there about Pelias. The bystanders were impressed with his beauty and stature, yet there was some hesitation in their answers. They were anxious not to be heard speaking against the king, whom they feared but did not love.

At that very moment, there was a cry from the outskirts of the crowd. People fell apart from Jason, not quite liking to be seen with him, and through the open space came King Pelias, driving furiously as was his custom. When the king's eye fell on the gigantic youth with one sandal who stood alone in his path, his heart turned over in his breast, and he jerked on the reins till the mules stopped in a cloud of dust. Yet he concealed his fear and called to the young man, "Who are you, stranger? You seem to be of the race of heroes. Tell me truthfully and do not be afraid."

The young man answered boldly and in few words. "Jason is my name and I am Aeson's son. I have come to claim my kingdom."

At that Pelias knew the danger that he had to meet, but since they were in the open marketplace, he smiled a false welcome with his lips and said: "For a long time I have waited for you, my cousin. I grow old and weary; you see my hair is grey. Yet I have no son of my own to whom I may entrust the kingdom; there is only you. Come to the palace then, and let me feast you while I send a message to your father. If you prove worthy, as you seem to be, I will give you the kingdom and go to live with Aeson, whose happiness I have envied all these years."

Jason answered in friendly fashion, since he was not usually suspicious. Accordingly the two went to the palace, and a great feast was set. Old Aeson was fetched from his retirement, while all the cousins of Jason, kings from the cities round, came over to welcome the young man, and they all marveled at his beauty and his gallantry. "He should be a great hero," they said to one another. Jason heard the flattery, for Pelias saw to it that he heard, and his heart was filled with joyous affection, even towards the king. It seemed to him that the intentions of Pelias must be honest, since he entertained him thus and made him known to his kin.

The feast went on for several days, during which no word was said of the kingdom between Pelias and Jason. But when the crafty king saw that he had won the young man's confidence, he took his chance to speak to him openly among some witnesses, saying: "It is high time, cousin Jason, that you took possession of the kingdom that is yours. I have kept it safe for long and weary years. Now at last my struggles are over, and I wish you better fortune, though I fear for you since there is a curse on all our kin. Only a great hero can remove it, and I had hoped when I was younger to gain the glory for myself. Alas, a king is not free to win glory. He must stay at home and struggle for his people. Would that I had been free to do great deeds when I was young!"

"What is this deed?" asked Jason loudly, for he was drunk with the flattery and anxious to show his powers. "I am young, and I am free if you will guard my kingdom for me. I will do this great deed and come again to Iolcos for my inheritance."

Pelias smiled to himself, but he pretended to be reluctant. He heaved a sigh. "It is hard for me to put off the time of retirement," he said. "Nevertheless, if you can do this mighty deed, why should I not give up a few of my declining years to help your fame? Our grandfather's brother, Athamas, and his wife, Ino, brought the curse on our kin. Here is the story. One day as Athamas was hunting, he heard a noise of laughter and came upon three maidens bathing in a mountain pool. On the bank lay their garments, and they themselves were playing in the water, clad only in their long, dusky hair. After watching them awhile, Athamas stole down to the grassy edge and took the clothes of one. Therefore when the two older sisters put on their misty garments and floated away into the air (for they were cloud nymphs), the youngest nymph could not depart with them. Athamas would not give her the robe, for all her begging and praying, until she promised to be his wife. Accordingly Nephele, the cloud nymph, married Athamas and bore him a son and a daughter, Phrixus and Helle.

"Fair though she was, however, she was too quiet and distant for her husband, who after long years began to grow tired of her. He fell in love with a proud and passionate mortal maiden, Ino, and Nephele left him in anger for the sky which is her home. Thereupon Athamas married Ino and made her queen of the land.

"Queen Ino loved Athamas, but, wishing to have the kingdom for her own sons, she hated Phrixus and Helle with a mortal hatred. When Hera in anger at the rejection of her servant, Nephele, sent a famine to the land, Ino saw her chance. Secretly she sent a vast bribe to the priestesses of Apollo's oracle, so that when Athamas asked how he might avoid the famine, they returned the false answer which she had suggested to them. To avoid the famine, they said, Phrixus and Helle must be slain in sacrifice to the gods.

"Athamas was appalled by the order, yet since men

were dying throughout the countryside, he did not dare to disobey. A great altar was set up; the priests came robed and crowned with the sacred woolen bands; the trembling children were led out to be slain. Lo, at that moment the gods listened to the prayers of Nephele and sent a rescuer. A great ram with a fleece of gold, shining like the sun, descended to them and took them on his back. Far up into the air it sped with them, Phrixus clasping its horns and Helle with her arms round her brother's waist.

"Over mountain and valley they flew at dizzy height, and the wind whistled round them as they clung. At last they passed over the narrow sea which separates Europe from Asia. When the weary, frightened Helle looked down and saw blue water far below, in her terror she let go her hold and dropped. In memory of her, Greeks call that strait the Hellespont. But Phrixus hung on and at last alighted in the land of Colchis, far off on the shores of the Black Sea. There the king welcomed him, giving him wealth and honor, and there he lived in happiness until a good old age. The golden ram they sacrificed in thankfulness for his safe arrival, and its glistening fleece hangs among the treasures of that king to this day.

"This, now, is the curse that hangs over us because of the crimes of Ino and Athamas. Until the golden fleece is brought back to the land from whence it came, the spirit of Phrixus will find no rest and misfortune will dog us. Some hero must sail to far Colchis across the dangerous seas to fetch the fleece, so that the spirit of Phrixus may return to his own land with it and there have rest."

Thus Pelias spoke, and the color of Jason mounted high, for his heart was on fire at the thought of mighty deeds. "I will go," he cried, "if you will keep my kingdom. It is a voyage for a hero. Who will come with me?"

"I will come" . . . "And I" . . . "And I" . . ., answered the young men in chorus, swept away by the heat of Jason and the desire for immortal fame.

2 . The Voyage of the Argo

In time the mightiest living heroes came from all over Greece to join the heroic crew. Argos, the great ship-builder, made their boat. They named it the *Argo* after him, and called themselves the Argonauts, or sailors of the *Argo*. Day after day the shipyard of Iolcos rang with blows of hammers. Day after day heroes poured into the little town. There were Orpheus, the great musician, King Admetus, Heracles himself with his bow-bearer, Hylas, and many others. The halls of the king were full of lights and singing as he feasted the heroes, entertaining them with stories of brave deeds done before. Pelias sat among them smiling a pleased and cunning smile, for he thought of the years of voyaging before them, and the chance that none of them would come home. His heart was light for the present as he drank to his cousin, Jason, wishing him riches and renown.

At last when the *Argo* was finished, the heroes dug a trench for her in the sand, and guiding her on the rollers, they slid her into the sea. They laid the mast and oars in her, while on the beach they killed two oxen as a sacrifice and made a great feast until the sun went down. When morning came, they leaped into the ship and took their places at the rowing benches. Men poured wine into the sea as an offering, the heroes struck with the oars, and the sea was churned white behind them. As they passed by the headland, there stood the old centaur, Cheiron, waving to them and wishing them safe return. Tears came into their eyes as they gazed for the last time on their land. At that Orpheus stood up in the bow with his lyre and sang to speed the rowers until shining fish pressed close behind to listen as his marvelous voice rang out across the water. Quickly the heroes reached the open sea, where they stepped the mast, spread the square sail upon it, and sped away from land.

Day after day they journeyed. Many were the islands to which they came. In some they found great kings who treated them nobly, but as the seas grew stranger, the lands became savage. Once they had to fight with monstrous giants, and another time as Hylas, the beautiful young bow-bearer of Heracles, bent over a stream to drink, he was seen by some river nymphs, who clasped their white arms around him and drew him in. Heracles then left the heroes to go hunting for his lost comrade and did not return. In another island the Argonauts fought with the Harpies, winged bird-women, who snatched the food from the tables and befouled what was left with a horrible smell that lingered wherever they had been. At last the heroes came to a narrow strait which led between the Clashing Rocks.

The Clashing Rocks were tall, jagged cliffs, not rooted in the soil as cliffs should be, but moving back and forth like the jaws of some vast monster. They closed together with a hideous crash and a thunder of boiling spray. Then they rebounded while the water seethed between them and their black rocks dripped with foam. Twice the men of the *Argo* saw the jaws close with a dreadful snap. Twice as the thunder died, they beheld the narrow path and the boiling seas between. Then to tempt the magic rocks, Jason bade let fly a dove swift as an arrow between the black, jagged teeth toward the blue water beyond. Slowly at first the wet rocks began to close, but soon they gathered speed as the gleaming bird sped through. They clashed again behind her, catching her tail feathers as she fled for her life through the roaring spray. Even as the crash came, the helmsman shouted, and the rowers drove with all their might into the midst of the seething waters. Around and over the ship fell a shower of blinding spray, but the heroes rowed for their lives in the whirling currents. They drove the *Argo* on so fast that she was grazed on either side by the slowly opening jaws.

Only the helmsman had eyes for the rocks, as they ground to a stop and gradually began to close. He saw them and called to the frantic oarsmen, for he caught a glimpse also of the calm sea beyond. The oars bent with the strain as the *Argo* flew for the opening. It seemed to the helmsman that she was too late, and so she would have been but that she was caught by the great wave of water pushed out by the closing rocks. Suddenly she was lifted high and spewed out headlong, while hardly an arm's length behind came the grinding clash. The spray fell over the Argonauts once more, but they were now safe and rowed far on to seek a harbor for that night.

They journeyed many days more, meeting many adventures. One hero died hunting a boar; some died of sickness. They passed the land of the Amazons, who are women warriors. They came to the land of the Chalybes, who did not keep flocks or plough but toiled year-long in underground mines and in the smoke of smelting houses. Once they were attacked by the birds of Ares, whose feathers were arrows of brass and who were proof against mortal weapons. From these too they escaped and sailed on past many strange harbors, until they came to the far distant land of Colchis and anchored at the mouth of its stream.

At Colchis Jason took counsel with his comrades. "Let us leave the ship at anchor in the river," he said, "where we can if need be escape to sea. I and a few of my comrades will go up to that city which you see through the morning mist, and there seek out King Aeetes and tell him frankly why we have come. If he consents, we will buy the fleece with rich gifts and promises of service; but if not, we may openly challenge him to fight."

The counsel seemed good to the others, and thus as the bright sun climbed higher, a little group of them, golden and splendid in their armor, passed through the crowds of dark-eyed Colchians in the marketplace and made their way up to the palace to speak with the king.

Aeetes had powers of dark magic, and his palace was a storehouse of many wonderful and terrible things. Green blossoming vines surrounded it with shade, while beneath them four fountains of milk, wine, oil, and water sent their colored columns dancing in the air. Wide were the carven gates, stately and round the pillars, and high the marble steps that the heroes had to climb. The tall, dark king was impressive as he came into the hall to meet the strangers. Aeetes greeted them in formal words, bade them be seated, and asked them whence they came. But Jason's glance slid away from him a moment, passed round the gorgeous hall and the rows of curious faces, and looked for a second full into the great, dark eyes of the king's daughter, who was gazing at him entranced.

The princess Medea was black-haired and slender. Gold girt her brown arms and bordered her long skirt. On her dark brows rested a tall, golden crown, while around her neck hung a curious symbol like a coiling snake with red eyes which flashed as she moved. For Medea was priestess of Hecate, the grey witch goddess, whose arms are wreathed with snakes, whose magic is performed in black night to the light of smoking torches, who comes riding through the darkness attended by the howling dogs of hell. Terrible were the sights that Medea had seen and dreadful were many of her secrets. The love that sprang up in her heart for the gigantic, blue-eyed hero was a savage love. As their eyes met, Jason felt her eagerness and something more. For all her fire and beauty, a cold feeling crept over him, so that with a start he looked away and caught the last words of King Aeetes.

Aeetes burned with anger as he heard the heroes' request, though he controlled his face and made no sign. In the first place he was far from willing to give up the marvelous treasure, and in the second he did not believe that the heroes would be content with that. He took them for pirates and thought that if he granted one demand, they would come back with another. Yet the men were clearly strong, and his spies reported the ship to be a great one. He thought a moment before he answered them.

"I will give you the fleece if you are worthy," he said at last. "But if you would have it, you must also be able to do what I can do. I have two oxen in my stalls, a gift of Ares. Their hooves are heavy with bronze and their nostrils breathe red fire. These I can harness and with them I plow Ares' sacred field into straight, black furrows. As I go, I sow my seed, the teeth of a dragon. The crop springs up behind me as the sun grows hot. From each tooth grows a warrior fully armed. For the reaping, I do battle with them single-handed and cut them down before the setting of the sun. If you can do as much, the fleece is yours."

The face of Jason grew grave, for he had not Aeetes' magic arts and knew he could not do the deed. Nevertheless he put a good face on the matter and answered proudly, "Send me your dragon's teeth and set a day. I will plow your field and reap it or die in the attempt."

Aeetes was filled with silent triumph as they parted, but Jason and his comrades were in despair. Most wished to refuse the challenge and declare open war, but Jason would not give in. As they sat on the deck disputing, there came a messenger from Medea to appoint a secret meeting place. At this the arguments broke out anew. The men had seen the princess' eyes on Jason and knew that if the hero would, he could win help from her. Most, however, thought it unworthy to encourage a woman to treachery against her father. Jason himself was for the meeting. In his own heart the princess still made him uneasy, yet he was not too proud to accept aid from a woman, provided it were given in secret. He did not love the girl, but she was beautiful. To accept her help was the easiest, indeed the only way.

Thus he quieted his fears and went to the meeting. When he returned, he said nothing of the passion of the wild princess and of the vows he had made to her, but he brought a box of ointment that she had given him. In the middle of the night he made a sacrifice to Hecate in the dark woods and anointed himself all over when he heard the howling of the goddess' ghostly hounds. He even smeared his shield and spear, making them and himself unconquerable for one day. Then he went to meet his fate.

When King Aeetes came down to the field of Ares to see his bulls let into the pasture, he was smiling a little to himself. But when he saw the hero go up to them till the red fire from their nostrils played harmlessly on his arms and shoulders, dark anger came into his face. Jason seized one of the oxen by the horns, twisted it to its knees with more than human strength, and drew the great yoke across its shoulders. At that the king looked broodingly at his daughter, who did not return his glance. The king turned away and watched in silence while the huge animals, goaded by the spear, were forced to draw the first black furrow straight across the field. He said nothing during the hours of plowing, though the onlookers marveled at the struggle and the hero's untiring strength.

At last when the seed was sown and the men in flashing helmets grew in long lines from the earth, the king smiled again, for even magic strength must fail against so many. At that Jason lifted a huge stone from the corner of the field and hurled it with all his force into the waiting ranks. In a moment each earth-born warrior turned fiercely on his neighbor and fought with him to the death. The king scowled with certainty at Medea, for she alone knew the secret of the stone. The princess looked straight ahead of her and gave no sign.

At last the crop was mowed, and Jason came staggering away from the rows of dead. The king forced a smile to cover his anger and greeted him with praise. "Now indeed I know that you are a hero among heroes," he declared. "Few could have done that deed, and great shall be your reward. Let your companions take you back to the ship, for you are weary. Tomorrow we will feast you and pay you as you deserve." Aeetes said no word of the fleece, for he was determined not to give it up.

Jason was carried back to the ship by his cheering comrades, while Aeetes returned silently to his palace, plotting treachery and revenge. Secretly he set spies to work to find out if his daughter had met the strangers on the day before, and he swore a horrible oath as to what he would do if she proved to have betrayed him. Meanwhile Medea had seen her father's accusing look and knew his nature. Besides, she too had spies.

When she stole quietly out in the darkness that same night, the palace sentries thought nothing of it. As Hecate's priestess she often went into the black woods to gather herbs or pray to the dark witch who had taught her spells. No one watched her turn towards the harbor instead of to the wood.

Soon the watchmen on shipboard heard Medea call, and they rowed out to her, while others aroused the ship. Jason met her with all his company, and before them she cast herself into his arms crying, "Save me and save yourselves from my father, Aeetes. He plans treachery against you tomorrow and a terrible revenge on me. We must be gone quickly while it is still dark, but first I will show you how to steal the fleece and escape the serpent who guards it. It is yours, for you won it fairly, though Aeetes will never give it up. Swear me a solemn oath that you will take me with you. Promise that you will take me to Greece as your wife, since for your sake I have betrayed my father and fled from my home. Henceforth you must be my protector, for I have no other left. Swear it."

"I swear it," answered Jason quickly, for her eagerness fired him, and if he might have the fleece, he cared little what came after.

Once more the Argonauts put out a boat to shore, and Jason and Medea entered the dark wood alone. Deep within it on the trunk of a great oak tree was nailed the fleece, shining like red-hot coal. Red light flushed the face of Jason and flickered on the hair of Medea as she moved. It gleamed dully from the scales of the vast serpent who was coiled about the tree and raised his head hissing as the intruders came near. The little tune that Medea hummed to him was not very loud, but it went on and on with a dull, insistent sound. The serpent swayed his head in time with it while she stroked him with her wand. Lower and lower sank his head until very, very slowly it came to rest at the enchantress' feet. "Quickly," she whispered to Jason as he lifted down the fleece. The two stole softly from the wood with their shining treasure and left the cold serpent sleeping by the empty tree in the dark.

Meanwhile on the ship the oars were put out, and the men took their places at the benches. When the boat returned, the moorings were loosened, men bent their backs, and the *Argo* leaped forward silently, yet visible in the dark. She gleamed with the light of the golden fleece which Jason had nailed in triumph to the mast.

Then began a stern race as the *Argo* fled for her life from the vengeance of Aeetes. Very early in the morning

he had discovered his daughter's flight, and the news of the theft and of the *Argo*'s disappearance followed quickly. Aeetes put out to sea in his mightiest ships. He crammed them with men to row in relays. Soon they had the *Argo* in sight, and all day long they gained on her, while the frantic Jason urged on the rowers and Medea paced hour-long by the windy stern, measuring the narrowing distance with her eye. At last when darkness came, Medea in her desperation did a dreadful thing. She caused the death of her own brother by her witchcraft and scattered his body in pieces on the sea. Aeetes stopped his ships when he saw the horrible sight and bade them gather up the body of his son for burial. All that day they scoured the sea for the scattered limbs, while the *Argo* grew smaller and smaller in the distance. Savage Medea openly proclaimed her deed, but the heroes glanced at one another behind her back, and Jason felt again the strange dismay with which he had first met the eyes of the dark princess.

3. The Aftermath

None seemed so pleased to see his dear cousin as old King Pelias. There was a tremendous celebration as the Argonauts poured into the little town. Neighboring kings came to see the fleece and to speak with the heroes who had brought it home. There were many joyful reunions. One by one the heroes said good-bye to Jason and set off for their homes. Still the feasting went on in the palace of Pelias. Jason seemed the most famous hero in the world; he was dizzy with praise. It was Medea who spoke to him finally, Medea, brooding, foreign, and ill-liked by the gay crowds.

"Jason," she said, "when are you to be king in Iolcos? What has Pelias said?"

Now for the first time Jason noticed that Pelias had said nothing. Embarrassed, he tried to put off Medea, but she returned to the subject day after day, till at last Jason was forced to take up the matter with Pelias himself.

Pelias was smooth and elusive. "For myself, you know it is my dearest wish," he said. "But there are the townsfolk. A foreign queen . . . Soon she will be used to our ways, and there may be less talk. Perhaps in a month or two . . ."

Jason waited a month or two, then a month or two more. There certainly was talk. But whether the delay was due to Pelias or the townspeople, he never could be quite sure. Medea blamed Pelias, and when Jason did nothing she determined to mend matters for herself. She became friendly, therefore, with Pelias' unmarried daughters and offered to teach them magic spells. Accordingly one day she took a poor old goat and killed it. She put it into a cauldron and boiled it with some herbs. Then she spoke magic words to it, and with that the goat leaped out of the cauldron far younger and more vigorous than he had been before. She showed the sisters how to do it.

"It will work with people too," she added casually.

"Really? Truly?" said the silly girls.

"Of course," she answered. "Now you are enchant-resses. You can give new youth to anyone you love who is feeling the burden of age." She had noticed that King Pelias was suffering from rheumatism.

Medea did not actually mention King Pelias, but the sisters went home and killed their father. When they put him in the cauldron and said spells over him, naturally he did not come to life. Unfortunately for Medea, the outrageous deed so aroused the citizens of Iolcos that they chased Jason and his wife away from the kingdom. Thus instead of helping her husband, Medea merely forced him into exile. Quarrels arose between the two. Medea clung to Jason as her only protector, and Jason still dreaded her as much as he loved her, regarding her now not as his helper, but as his misfortune. While her violent deeds had been done in Colchis, he could profit by them and forget them. Here in Greece he could do neither. Therefore the deeds themselves seemed uglier to him.

Then passed some years of bitterness until at last Creon, king of Corinth, with whom the pair had taken refuge, persuaded Jason to get rid of his foreign wife. In her stead he offered his own daughter, being glad to gain a son-in-law who was still very famous, even though the years since his great adventure had brought him little good. Jason for his part was ready to marry the young princess and to be rich once more and the heir to a kingdom. He felt people might believe in him again if he got rid of the foreign witch. He persuaded himself that he would give her money and help their two sons to rise in the world when he himself became great. With such thoughts he comforted himself, and in fear of Medea took once more the easy way. Arrangements were made in secret, the match was hurried on, and not until the very eve of the wedding was Medea told.

Her rage and grief were terrible. All night and all day she wept, thinking now of her far distant home, her murdered brother, the father she had betrayed, now of the hatred she had met from all in Greece for Jason's sake. She thought of the terrible things she had done for him, of her magic powers, of the terrible things she still could do. She groaned aloud, crying curses on the princess and on King Creon, and most of all on Jason, who had broken his oath to her. Helpless servants watched her from the doorway, afraid to come in, yet unwilling to leave her. They thought she might do herself injury, and they were frightened by her wild words and the fierce looks she gave Jason's children, her little sons.

Nevertheless, after a time Medea seemed to pull herself together. When King Creon, alarmed by the news of her fury, decided to banish her from his land, she asked only one day's grace to find a place of refuge. When Jason came at last to offer her money that she might not go away penniless, she controlled herself enough to make him a request. She prayed him to take their children and bring them up as princes in his new household. To gain the consent of the young bride, she offered to send her a message of good will and a royal gift. Jason sighed with relief as a man who is rid of a tiresome burden. Gladly he gave his consent to the gift for the princess. Thereupon Medea sent her a casket beautifully adorned with figures of beaten gold. Within lay a marvelous robe, fine as silk yet heavy with embroidery, which Medea had taken out of her secret treasure chest. From the same chest she sent a tall, golden crown such as she herself used to wear in her days of splendor.

The little princess clapped her hands with delight when she saw the costly gifts. She jumped up from her seat at once to put on the gorgeous robe. Then she ran over to the mirror and fitted the tall crown carefully upon her shining head. She paraded up and down for a moment, chattering to her servants and looking over her shoulder at her image. Suddenly she stopped, looking pale and dizzy. She put up her hands and tugged at the crown; it would not come off. She tried to fling off the robe, but it clung to her like a cobweb. Then with a shriek she fell writhing onto the couch as Medea's poison passed like fire through her veins, and she died, crying out in horrible agony, while the terrified servants stood by in helpless panic. Her old, grey father came rushing in to snatch the fiery garment from her, but he could neither remove it nor tear himself away so that he too perished miserably. The maddened Jason rushed from the palace to take vengeance on Medea, but he was already too late. Over the roof of their house she hovered in the air, riding in a chariot drawn by dragons. At her feet lay the bodies of their little sons.

Jason was beside himself. "Fierce witch, unnatural mother, tigress, not woman," he cried to her. "How could you murder your own children? Had you no pity for them?"

"Pity for them, yes," she cried, "but hate for you. I made you a hero. I brought you the golden fleece. For this I gave up my country, my father, and every friend I knew. Only one thing I asked of you, that you should be faithful, and you swore it. Ask the heroes of the *Argo* if you have forgotten. They will remember."

"You drove me from my home in Iolcos," he flung back at her.

"I killed your enemy for your sake as I had done before. You left me fatherless and friendless in a foreign land. Now you too are homeless, wifeless, childless; my injuries are avenged."

"But not mine," he threatened her.

"I am beyond your vengeance. I shall go to Athens where the king is a protector of the weak. Because I am homeless and helpless, he will keep me safe. I shall think of you often in the long years to come and be glad of my revenge."

The dragon chariot sailed off into the air. The ruined man watched it go. Now he was neither rich nor heir to a kingdom. He was no longer admired as a hero, since Medea's terrible vengeance had been, as all knew, provoked by his conduct. The days of Jason's fame were over; he did no deed thereafter of which the minstrels sing.

VII
GREAT HEROES

Theseus

1. The Youth of Theseus

Two Greek heroes, Heracles and Theseus, had many adventures, not just one, and were famous for their characters as much as for their achievements. Heracles was the outstanding example of physical strength and fitness. Theseus was the wise, just ruler. Each of them therefore stood for something which the Greeks greatly admired. These are the best of the many stories about them.

Theseus was brought up by his mother, Aethra, in her father's palace in the little kingdom of Troezen. It was a quiet, pleasant household where the boy learned to associate kindness and justice with the office of a king. Aethra saw to it that he was educated in running, jumping, wrestling, throwing the discus and javelin, boxing, swordplay, and all the skills of a prince. He was taught also to love poetry and music. Wandering minstrels came to the palace singing of the great deeds of old. At the same time they brought news of the world as it was then, of greater kingdoms less pleasantly ruled than Troezen, of lawlessness, robbery, injustice, and of the heroes of Theseus' own time who fought against these evils. Aethra encouraged her son to listen, for she said he was a great prince and must take thought for these things. Yet when the boy asked her of his father, she would tell him nothing. She always answered that he must be patient until the time came for him to learn the truth.

The years went by and the boy became a youth fired with ambition to be worthy of a great destiny. At last he went to his mother one birthday and said to her, "Mother, I am now a man. Tell me about my father, for I am old enough to seek him out and to take my place in the world."

Aethra looked at her son thoughtfully, taking in the brown arms, the steady blue eyes, the upright carriage, and the slender, athletic form that had not yet come to its full strength. "Perhaps it is time," she said at last. "Come with me and we will see."

Mother and son walked together up a pleasant hill towards a little grove of trees. As they went, the quiet voice of Aethra spoke of the daily tasks of the household, just as though this were an ordinary day and she had nothing to tell her son. When they came to the summit, she showed him a great, grey stone lying flat on its side half buried in the clinging grass.

"Lift up that stone for me if you can," she said quietly.

Theseus bent down to the stone and strained at it with all his strength. First he tried it from one side and then from the other. Finally he stood up and wiped his

brow for a moment while he had a look at it. Then he
dug a little of the earth away with his fingers to get a
better grip and tore at it till it seemed as though his back
would break, but it was no good. He might just as well
have tried to lift a mountain for all the success he had.

"Never mind, my son," said the gentle Aethra. "Next
year we will try again." She walked back towards the
palace with her arm in her son's, talking calmly of other
things.

Next year when his birthday came, Theseus went up
once more with his mother to lift the mighty stone. This
time he stirred it a little from its bed, and had it not been
sunk so deeply in the earth, he might have raised it.

"Never mind, my son," said Aethra once more. "We
can wait another year."

This was his second failure, and Theseus determined
that the third time, come what would, he must lift that
stone. All day long he was out-of-doors, running,
wrestling, exercising, even helping his grandfather's
servants harvest the grain, carrying the heavy baskets
of grapes to the winepress, and doing whatever hard
work he could find. Therefore, when they walked up
the hill again, mother and son were silent, for they
knew the great day was come and each felt glad and
sorry for the parting that lay ahead.

They looked down from the hilltop still in silence at
the harbor, the quiet town, the few miles of pasture and
plowland, and the uplands of scrub and heather which
made up the little kingdom of Troezen. Far off to the
north lay purple lines of rocky hills, pathless, and dan-

gerous, but near at hand it was early summer and everything was green. Theseus and his mother stood there for a moment, listening to the distant baaing of goats and the calls of children, while the birds sang in the branches above them, bees hummed in the grass, and the warm sunlight fell across the stone. Then Theseus strode quickly across to it, got his fingers beneath, and with a mighty heave raised it first knee high, then to his shoulder, and with a final gasp rolled it clear over onto its back in triumph. Beneath the stone, kept safe in a little hollow that had been scooped out for them many years before, lay a pair of sandals and a sword.

Theseus gathered up the treasures and turned back to his mother. "The time is come," he said to her. "Now tell me who is the father who left these things for me."

"He is Aegeus, king of Athens," Aethra answered him.

"Aegeus, king of Athens!" cried Theseus in exultation. "Aegeus, the lover of justice, the protector of the weak!"

"He said good-bye to me on this hilltop," said Aethra. "He rolled aside the stone himself and hid the sword and sandals beneath. Then he told me that if our child should prove a daughter, I was to keep her and bring her up and marry her well. If we had a son, I was to take him to this stone when he was grown a man and bid him roll it away. If he could not, I should keep him with me; but if he were strong enough, I should send him to Athens with the sandals and the sword that he might claim his inheritance."

"His inheritance," repeated Theseus softly. He slung the sword about him and with the sandals in his hand turned to his mother. "Let us go," said he.

"Yes, we will go," answered Aethra, "and tomorrow we will fit out a ship for you that you may travel like a prince."

"No, not by sea," said Theseus. "I shall travel by land, and alone."

"Alone and by land!" said Aethra quickly. "No, that can never be. By land the route is almost pathless. It is savage and lawless; robbers and strange monsters haunt it. No man travels by land, at least not alone."

"That is how I shall go," said Theseus firmly. "Is not Athens the city of justice, the refuge of the weak? I will destroy these robbers and monsters who rule the land. Thus when I come to my father, my fame will come with me and he will know that I am a worthy son."

Aethra begged her son to be reasonable, and her old father added his prayers, but it was no use. The next day Theseus put on the sandals, took his sword, kissed his mother, and walked quietly out of the palace toward the hills.

Athens is many days' journey to the north of Troezen, and, as Aethra had said, the way was perilous. Theseus was at home in the open, and he had a friendly word for the people in town or cottage wherever he came. Yet the hills were wild and lawless, so that he never knew whether a stranger was a peaceful shepherd or hunter or whether he was one of the fierce robbers who held the whole countryside in terror. One day a curious looking man stepped out of the wood onto the path in front of him in a lonely stretch of the road. At first sight he seemed quite dangerous. He was immensely shaggy with matted hair and beard. His shoulders were enormous, and he carried a huge club bound with iron. Yet from the waist down he was tiny, with little, crooked legs, and he came shuffling along the path calling out in a high, nasal voice to the noble young stranger to have pity on a poor cripple and give him money. Theseus let him come near, thinking him harmless, but when he was within arm's length he reared up and struck a blow with the massive club which would have dashed Theseus' brains out if he had not been young and quick. As it was, the youth jumped aside just in time, and, as the man swayed for a moment overbalanced by the force of his own stroke, he snatched out his father's sword and stabbed the robber to the heart. He put back the sword in its sheath, took up the great club as a trophy of his first fight, and walked on. At the next village there was great excitement when people saw him carrying it. They crowded round to thank him and to tell him that the robber was named the Club Bearer and had terrorized innocent travelers for many years.

Theseus' next adventure was with a robber called Sinis, or the Pine Bender, because he bent down to earth the tops of two pine trees and tied his prisoners between them. Then he let go, and the trees sprang upright again with a terrific force, tearing the poor wretches apart. Sinis rushed at Theseus with a mighty weapon made from the trunk of a pine tree, but strong as he was, Theseus was stronger, and the iron-bound club was superior to the pine. The Pine Bender was vanquished and came to the miserable end he had often prepared for others.

Theseus traveled on, and now his fame spread before him far and wide until people came down to the way to meet him, both to speak with a great hero and to beg him to deliver them from trouble. In this way Theseus was persuaded to kill the great wild boar of Crommyon which was laying waste the countryside. Then he came upon the dreadful Sciron, who sat by the road where it passed over a steep cliff by the sea and forced all passers-by to wash his feet. As the trembling victim was busy with his task, Sciron kicked out and tumbled him backwards over the cliff onto the rocks below. Theseus gave him, too, a dose of his own medicine and passed on to another place where he killed a great wrestler by dashing him to the ground.

By now even in the remotest parts, people would come to greet Theseus and thank him for rescuing them. Therefore he was not surprised when one evening a man stepped out onto the road in a lonely spot and offered him shelter for the night. He was a queer man, though; he was very tall and thin with a pale face and pale eyes that never stood still for a second. He shuffled his feet and cracked his fingers. Everything about him was jerky except his voice, which was smooth as oil. "You do my poor home honor," he kept on saying. "So great a hero! So poor a shelter! Yet perhaps you are wise. Many great and noble men have spent the night with me." He laughed, not very loud but on and on, as though at a joke of which he was never weary.

"Where is your house?" said Theseus shortly, for he saw no point in laughing and he did not like the man. "Perhaps it is too far. I must be on my road at dawn."

"Ah no," said the strange man quickly. "It is not far. Just over the hill. In ten minutes, in five minutes if the noble hero is willing, we shall be at the door. Just five minutes from the highway! Think how easy. Yet of all the noble strangers who have rested in my bed, not one has roused himself to be on the roadway in the dawning. So sound a sleep! And dreamless! It is a noble bed!" He laughed again and jerked a hand onto Theseus' arm above the elbow as if to guide him. The grip was surprisingly strong. The youth suffered himself to be hurried up a rocky path, for he thought he knew the man now from stories that he had heard, and he was anxious to see what he would do.

At last they came in sight of a mean hovel roughly piled together in the midst of the rocks. "Come in, come in," said the stranger quickly, pulling a little harder at his arm. "Come and rest. Did I tell you I have a bed for you? You are very tall, yet my bed will fit you. Oh yes, it will fit!"

Theseus pulled his arm free and turned on the man in the doorway. "I have heard of you," he said quietly. "Your bed is a hard plank and narrow, and it needs no blankets. Yet all men exactly fit it, so they say, and

when they are laid upon it, they sleep very soundly in death. Is not your name Procrustes?"

Procrustes turned upon him and grasped his arm again. "Better men than you," he cried, "have fitted my dreadful bed. For if a man be too short when he is laid thereon, I stretch him till he fits it. But if he be too long, I shorten him with the knife. Now you shall lie, my young hero, where so many better men have lain before. You are tall for my bed at present, but it will fit you yet."

With that he threw his arms about Theseus and made as though to lift him. But the hero burst the grip with a mighty heave and seized him by the waist. Then he lifted him to his shoulder and bore him struggling through the dark doorway. Accordingly as night fell, Theseus set forth once more upon his road in the dark, leaving Procrustes stretched upon the terrible bed which had fitted all other men and now at last fitted him.

2. The Minotaur

Meanwhile at Athens the long reign of King Aegeus was coming to an inglorious end. The whole land was split by quarrels between Aegeus' cousins, who considered themselves his heirs, while the old king himself was completely under the sway of the witch, Medea, to whom he had given protection when Corinth drove her out. Even the common people were tired of Aegeus, for he had been defeated in war by Minos of Crete, and the land was forced to pay a dreadful tribute every nine years. Theseus preferred to make no claim on the aged king. He came as a mighty hero who happened to be traveling through Athens and asked the king to receive him as a guest, thinking that his likeness to Aethra would cause the old man to recognize his son.

Aegeus agreed to receive the hero, since he could hardly refuse the request of such a famous man, but Medea, the enchantress, who had learned who Theseus was, had already whispered to him that the young man was a traitor who came to seize his throne. The feeble old king, confused by her dark spells and made suspicious by the constant intrigues around him, believed her. Medea smiled to herself, for she knew that if Theseus were recognized by his father, her reign in Athens would be at an end.

A great crowd of people poured out to meet Theseus at the gates of the city and escorted him with shouts and cheering to the palace of the king. More and more came hurrying from house and dock and workshop, wriggling their way into the crowd to catch sight of him, or standing on tiptoe on the outskirts to get a glimpse of the hero's head as it towered above the rest. Even the palace servants ran out at last, and the old king pressed his thin lips together as he saw them go, while his scanty grey beard quivered with his indignation.

"He is indeed a traitor," he said to Medea. "He steals my very servants from before my eyes."

Medea smiled at him. "I will deal with him," she

said. "Let us go out on the steps to welcome him. We
will greet him with honor and bid him come in. When
he enters the hall, do you sit him down and call for meat
and wine. I myself will pour his wine for him; he shall
drink from my golden cup. There are poisons I have
brought from Colchis that the witch-goddess helped me
brew. Let him take but one sip that I shall pour for him,
and he will never claim your throne."

The old king nodded feebly, for he was half crazed
by her spells. "Do not fail with the poison," he qua-
vered, "and now help me to the door."

They stood on the steps to greet the hero, the slender, dark-eyed sorceress, and the tottering old man
leaning on her arm. Theseus turned from the witch in
anger, but he looked his father in the face. The old man
had forgotten Aethra; he did not know her son. He
bade Theseus welcome formally and invited him within,
but he gave no sign of recognition, and the hero followed him wondering.

The traveler was bathed and dressed for feasting.
Tables were set up within the hall. Meat was brought in
by the servants. Wine and water were mixed in huge
bowls. Each guest was brought a wine cup of red earthenware on which a skillful artist had painted some deed
of a hero of whom the minstrels sang. Medea would not
let Theseus drink from his.

"You are our guest of honor," she said. "You shall
drink from gold, and a king's daughter shall serve you."
With that she fetched him wine in a curious golden cup
such as the great artists of Crete had made.

Theseus took the cup and turned to his father, for he had a mind to drink his health in it. The old king was looking at him in a fixed silence, while his fingers drummed nervously on the table. There was something so unpleasant about his stare that Theseus was startled, and the first hint of treachery came into his mind. He determined to test his father. Therefore he kept his left hand on the winecup, but with his right instead of a knife he drew out his father's sword and made as though he would cut himself a portion of the meat with it. Seeing that sword, the king reached out startled, snatched the winecup from Theseus' hand, and dashed it to the floor. Then he jumped up and flung his arms about the young man, calling him son. For her part, Medea, seeing her treachery was discovered and knowing that her reign was over, vanished from Athens and was seen no more.

Aegeus proudly acknowledged his son and named him as his heir, but the king's cousins, who were not pleased at this, stirred up the common people against King Aegeus. It happened to be the time when the tribute to Minos became due. Seven youths and seven maidens were chosen by lot from among the people to go to Crete as a sacrifice to the dreadful monster, the Cretan Minotaur. What happened to them when they got there no one knew, for no one who once went in had ever come out of the famous labyrinth that Daedalus had made for the beast to dwell in. Men could hear the distant bellowing of the monster in his lair, and it was supposed he ate up his victims, though some said they became priests in his temple. At any rate, because their children were chosen by lot for a dreadful fate, the people were furiously indignant. So too was Theseus when he heard the tale.

"Why has no one dared to slay this Minotaur?" he asked King Aegeus. "This is no way to pay tribute. Let me go to Crete and put an end to it."

"No, my son," said King Aegeus terrified. "No one can slay the Minotaur, for the young men are not allowed to take any weapons as they go into the labyrinth. Besides, the victims are chosen from the people, and you are not of the people; you are the king's son."

"All the more reason I should go," said Theseus. "I shall not wait to be chosen. I shall volunteer."

The king implored him with tears in his eyes, but Theseus was determined, and the people idolized him more than ever when they heard what he was to do. The ship made ready for the chosen victims was small and quite unarmed, as the terms of the treaty bade. She had a black sail of mourning, that all might know that she bore the tribute to King Minos and must be allowed to pass. This time Theseus bade them put in a white sail as well. "When we return," he said, "we shall come with open rejoicing as a free people should."

The ship put off from the bay and the weeping people watched it go. King Aegeus sat on the headland looking after it, and there, he told his son, he should watch daily until the ship came home. But the chosen youths and maidens, encouraged by the cheerfulness of Theseus, sang songs to cheer their journey across the sea. When they came to the great wharves of the town of Cnossos, they put on a bold face. Even the powerful ships of Minos did not dismay them, or the sight of his huge stone palace, or the crowds of townsfolk who came down to watch the tribute come to land.

Many a man felt pity as he saw the handsome youth at the head of the little group and heard that he was the king's only son and that he was a volunteer. There was talk of granting him a weapon that he might have a fair chance against the Minotaur, but King Minos would not hear of it. The challenge of Theseus only made him angry.

"How dare you come here in defiance?" he said to the young man. "Tomorrow we will throw you to the monster and we shall see what your boast is worth."

"I dare because the tribute is unjust," replied Theseus firmly. "Armed or unarmed I will fight your hideous bull-man. If I prevail, I warn you, O Minos, that we Athenians are a free people and the tribute shall cease. If I die, I die; but the tribute is still unjust."

Some murmured admiration at his boldness, but King Minos stood up from his throne in wrath. "Take his sword," he ordered his guards, "and lock the victims in the dungeons over night. Tomorrow we will give you to the Minotaur, and after that the tribute will go on. The black-sailed ship shall return to Aegeus to tell him that he has no son. The Athenians need to remember that the sea is mine, and, distant as they are, they must live in dread of my power."

The guards closed in on the Athenians and took

them down to the cold, dark dungeons. People watched them pityingly, for they knew Theseus had no chance, yet they admired the handsome young man who spoke so boldly before them all. None pitied him so much, however, as the soft-hearted king's daughter, white-footed Ariadne. She had heard Theseus speak in the hall as she stood beside her father, her bright hair about her shoulders and a great crown flashing with jewels upon her head. In the dead of night she left her chamber and stole on silent feet down the long, stone corridors toward the dungeons, quietly drew the great bolt, and went in.

She stood in the moonlight which fell through a high, little window, and Theseus thought she was some goddess at first, for her white feet were bare on the stone, there was gleaming gold on her scarlet garment, and the bright crown was still on her head. She bade Theseus rise and come with her, making no sound. "I will give you a sword," she whispered softly, "with which you may fight the Minotaur fairly and slay him if you can."

She took his hand to guide him in the long, dark passages, and together they stole down many corridors, past many a darkened door. At last they reached a little room from which ran a passage dimly lighted. From here they heard echoing faintly a low, hoarse bellowing sound.

"Here is the Labyrinth," said Ariadne. "Far off in the center lies the Minotaur. Bend down your ear to listen

while I whisper to you the secret clue Daedalus gave
my father that he might find the center of the Labyrinth. To return is not so easy. Many doors lead out
from the center; yet only one will bring you here. Take
this sword in your right hand and this ball of thread in
your left. We will tie the end of it to a pillar and you
may unwind it as you go. Then it will be easy to return
as you gather in the thread."

She gave him the thread and the sword, and
watched him out of sight. For a while she heard his
footsteps moving round and round within. At times
they stopped as though he stood puzzling before the
maze of passages, but then they went on again, and
presently they died away. She stood there for a long
time looking at the shining thread across the floor and
hearing the distant roaring which arose from the monster's lair. She heard when he reached the center,
because the roar grew suddenly louder and went on
and on. Then there fell a dead silence, and for a long
while nothing happened. If Theseus were dead or
wounded, she might wait till morning and he would
never come. It seemed hours that she had been standing, and the stone floor was very cold.

At last she thought she heard footsteps. Someone
twitched the line. The sounds came louder and clearer,
till Theseus emerged from the passage with the sword
red in his hand. She fell upon him eagerly.

"Why were you so long?" she whispered. "It must be
nearly dawn."

"It is a dreadful monster," he said in answer. He was still shaken by the sight of the horrible creature whom few living men had seen.

"Quickly, then!" she whispered. "We have not much time." Hand in hand they stole down the long corridors again, roused the group from their dungeon, and sped down to the little ship which was moored beside the wharf. There were urgent explanations in whispers, and then the sailors scrambled over one another to hoist the sail. Very quietly they cast her off, and shipped oars as soon as they dared. Then they fled for their lives as the sky grew pale with the first light before the dawn.

All day long they raced away in panic fearing pursuit from the great ships of the Cretan fleet. They had put up the black sail in the dark that morning, but when some spoke of it and bade them hoist the white one, the sailors refused to take the time. Frantically they rowed till they were exhausted, landing at last worn out on the island of Naxos, where they lay down to sleep. In the morning there was a false alarm of a sail on the horizon, and tumbling into their ship, they fled again. In vain Theseus called to them that Ariadne had been left sleeping on the beach. Even though they owed her their lives, they did not care. They were mad to reach Athens and safety.

Ariadne slept without waking till the ship was far out to sea, and then she wandered for a long time up and down, calling vainly for Theseus and the men who had forsaken her. At last the god, Dionysus, found her as he came to Naxos with his train and persuaded her to come up to the heavens and be his bride. To proclaim to all people that she had done so, he took her crown and set it in the heavens, where each jewel became a star, and where it can still be seen.

Theseus' terrified crew still raced toward Athens with no thought in their heads but speed. At last they came within sight of the headland on which King Aegeus sat, looking out over the blue ocean day after day for tidings of his son. Now when he saw the black-sailed ship, he was in despair, for he remembered the white sail they had taken with them and the words of Theseus that he would come back in freedom and rejoicing. The poor old man thought he had nothing to live for and, even while the joyful Theseus looked eagerly at the land, Aegeus threw himself over the cliff to perish in the sea.

Thus Theseus came to his throne with mourning instead of rejoicing. Thereafter he reigned long and his rule was a famous one. The Athenians told many stories of his justice, his kindness to the common people, and of the ways in which he made Athens great. Traditions speak of Theseus offering protection to people who had suffered injustice in other lands. Some even declare that he gave up the title of king, preferring to give power to the people.

There are also tales of his achievements in war; how he fought with the Amazons and won their queen to wife; how he battled with the centaurs; how he even went down to Hades in an unsuccessful attempt to carry off Persephone. There he was caught and imprisoned, and other people came to power in Athens. When he was finally rescued by Heracles, he never regained his power, but was driven out and died on the island of Scyros. Yet in spite of this the Athenians always spoke of him as a great king and patriot. When the mighty king of Persia tried to invade Athens in the year 490 B.C. and was defeated by its little army at the battle of Marathon, one of the famous battles of all time, then the rumor went around and the legend lingered that on that day of crisis the great Theseus, risen from the dead, had appeared to lead the battle.

Later still there was found on the island of Scyros a mighty skeleton, taller than most men and buried with bronze-headed spear and sword. Taking these for the bones of Theseus, the Athenians brought them home and buried them. From that day the tomb of Theseus was a place of refuge for poor men and slaves and all who had suffered wrong. While they were there, no man could harm them. In this way the Athenians honored the memory of the just hero who was kind to the oppressed.

Heracles

1. The Youth of Heracles

The first story about Heracles tells of his strength when he was less than a year old. One night his mother, Alcmena, fed him, bathed him as usual, and then put him to bed for the night with his twin brother, Iphicles, in a cradle made of a great bronze shield which their father, Amphitryon, had won in battle. She kissed the little boys lying close together, and rocked them gently for a time until they fell asleep. Presently she crept away, and not long after, the whole house lay silent and dark.

Now Zeus was the protector of Heracles, but his wife, Hera, had other favorites and was jealous. This night she sent two dark snakes silently coiling past the pillars of the house door, sliding across the floor towards the shield. Just as they reared their dark heads and coiled themselves up to strike, Zeus lit up the whole room with brightness, and at the warning the children awoke. When Iphicles saw the swaying heads peering at him over the rim of the shield, he screamed aloud in fright and kicked aside the blanket over him,

213

trying to pull himself over to the other side. Not so Heracles; he grasped the snakes by the neck in his fat baby hands and clutched with all his might.

In another moment all the house was in an uproar. The angry snakes whipped back and forward. They wound their coils about the baby's arms and tried to squeeze. But Heracles only gripped tighter and choked them till they could not hold on any more. In the next room, Alcmena leaped from bed, seeing it bright as daylight in the house and hearing the sounds of struggle and Iphicles screaming.

"Quick!" she gasped to her husband. "Quick! Get your sword!"

Amphitryon jumped up half awake and fumbled for the weapon that hung on a peg beside his bed. At that moment the bright light vanished. They could hear no more struggle. Only the sound of Iphicles' crying went lustily on and on.

"Lights! Lights!" Amphitryon shouted to his household. "Bring torches, unbolt the doors!"

People flocked into the room, Amphitryon first with his drawn sword in his hand, Alcmena close behind him, and the servants crowding with torches through the door. There in the cradle lay Iphicles, hushed now but white with fear. Beside him lay Heracles chuckling to himself as he held out his arms to his father, while in the two tiny fists lay the dead bodies of the snakes, choked to death by the strength of his grip.

Alcmena picked up Iphicles and comforted him, but Amphitryon merely tucked the blanket in again over

Heracles and let him go back to sleep. From that time on both parents knew that their child would be a mighty hero.

The youth of Heracles was spent in Thebes, where famous men taught him the skills that a hero should know. He learned poetry and music, but cared far more for sports, in which he excelled. He rode and ran, threw the javelin and wielded the spear. Above all he was famous as an archer and a wrestler and for his incredible strength. Indeed, even in his early youth he is said to have killed a man by accident, striking him too hard when he was in one of his rages. Yet he performed such services in war for Thebes that his fellow citizens soon forgave him, and the king gave him his own daughter to wife. Heracles was very happy with her for a while, but at last, the story says, in a fit of madness he killed both his wife and his three little sons, not knowing what he did.

None of the legends explain very well this terrible action of Heracles. Some say he went mad from rage at an injury done him and for a moment could not tell friend from foe. Others say this madness was sent on him by his old enemy, Hera. However it was, when he came to his senses Heracles most bitterly repented. Even though he had not known what he was doing, for a long while he hid his face from other people and would not even speak to them. At last he asked the gods what he should do to pay for this terrible sin, and was told to bind himself for eight years as servant to King Eurystheus and to perform ten tasks for him.

This was a very hard punishment for Heracles. He
was a proud man, and besides King Eurystheus was a
weakling and a coward who was jealous of the great
hero and proceeded to give him the hardest tasks he
could find. Also he objected to two of the tasks Heracles performed because the hero had had help in one
and had earned a profit from another. Eventually,
therefore, instead of doing him ten services, Heracles
had to do twelve. These twelve are generally called the
Twelve Labors of Heracles and are the most famous
things he did. Several of them involved killing dangerous monsters, while for some of the others Heracles had
to take long journeys on which he did many brave
deeds for the people into whose lands he came. Thus
there are numerous stories about the services of Heracles to men, and of the glory and profit he won for
himself; the twelve labors are merely the ones that we
know best.

2 . The First Two Labors

The first of the twelve tasks given to Heracles was the
killing of the Nemean Lion. This great beast had his lair
near the sacred grove of Zeus at Nemea whence he rav-
aged the nearby countryside. Heracles took the great
bow that none but he could bend, and made himself a
mighty club from the trunk of an olive tree which he
tore up by the roots. With these weapons he went up
the valley toward the rocky cleft where the beast was

supposed to live. It was noon as Heracles passed
through Nemea, finding no track of the monster and
hearing no sound of roaring. Though it was midday, the
whole place seemed deserted. No man was busy plowing, and the cattle strayed in the fields untended while
the inhabitants shut themselves up safe indoors. It was
better to lose a cow or a sheep than one's own life, and
from this beast not even the bravest man was safe.

Heracles passed through the silent valley and began
to climb the wooded hill as the sun sank low. Presently
he heard a rustling in the undergrowth. He made towards it, and as he came out onto a wide clearing, he
saw the lion. The lion was not in a warlike mood; it had
killed and eaten already and was now going home to
sleep. It was an enormous monster, and its great, hairy
face was dark with blood and streaked with dust. It
padded up the hill, head low, making for its den.

Heracles crouched down behind a group of bushes
fitting an arrow to the string. With all his strength he let
fly, and his aim was true. The arrow struck the lion full
in the side, but to the hero's amazement it simply
bounded off and fell on the grass. Then Heracles knew
that it was no ordinary lion. Nevertheless before the enraged beast could turn upon him, he shot again. Again
he hit, and again the arrow bounded off and was lost.
Before he could shoot a third time, the lion was on him
with a mighty spring. Heracles met him in midair. In his
left hand he held his folded cloak hastily flung over his
arm to break the force of the blow, but with the right he

raised his club and struck the lion full on the forehead
with such fearful force that the club broke clear in half
and he was left defenseless.

The lion dropped to the ground dazed. Were it not
for the bush of hair that protected his head, even his
huge skull might have been cracked. As it was, he still
stood on his four feet but blinded and staggering, shaking his great head slowly to and fro. Then with a quick
spring, Heracles was on his back and his arms were
about the lion's throat. In vain did the beast rear up and
rend the air with his claws then drop back and scrape
great furrows in the ground. In vain did he dash himself
from side to side. The man still clung, and the mighty
arms gripped ever more tightly round his throat. He
opened his mouth to roar, but no sound came forth. He
reared up again and this time was held there helpless
while his useless forepaws beat the air. At last his struggles grew fainter until finally he went limp. Heracles
had strangled him by main strength.

Heracles was immensely proud of his first achievement. He skinned the lion — no easy task to cut off that
iron hide — and went back to Eurystheus with the thing
slung about him as a cloak. The two forepaws fastened
it about his neck, and if he wanted, he could draw up
the lion's head over his own. He came swaggering into
the presence of Eurystheus, and that coward king, who
had hoped to get rid of Heracles and feared that the
hero knew it, was so terrified at the fierce lion's head
and the great man who carried it that he turned white

and trembled before the eyes of all his court. He quickly left the hall before Heracles could come near him, and the bold hero shouted with laughter, while the attendants whispered among themselves.

Eurystheus was furiously angry with Heracles, who had shown him up as a coward in everyone's sight; so the next time he determined to give him a task that he simply could not do. He told him to go and kill the Lernaean Hydra. This was a great swamp serpent with nine heads, one of which was actually immortal. It had such a dreadful poison that it infected the very air, and the whole region around it was deserted, for no one dared use the water from the springs near where it dwelt. This time Heracles did not go on his quest alone but took with him Iolaus, son of his twin-brother, Iphicles. Iolaus was still a boy, and his uncle took him not to help him against the Hydra, but to travel with him and to drive his chariot. The two rode across the deserted country where neither men nor beasts could dwell until they came to the springs of the river which welled out beside the Hydra's den.

Here Heracles left Iolaus with the horses and himself stepped forward and sent a few arrows whizzing into the darkness of the cave. He knew from the hissing within that he had roused the animal, and as it slithered forward out of the rock, he sprang upon it and dashed his club on the nearest flickering head. The head dropped crushed and shapeless as the long neck went limp, but the beast came coiling forward, eight heads still darting venomously. Heracles gave ground and lifted his club once more, but even as he did so, he saw the limp neck rouse again, and from its shattered end grew two new necks, and from each of these a head. Again he swung his club and again jumped back a pace, but once more the same thing happened. The second shattered head grew whole again and became not one head, but two.

Then the hero was desperate, for he saw that against this monster even his strength could not prevail alone. "Iolaus!" he shouted, "Iolaus!" not daring to look round and see whether the boy was still with the horses or whether he had run for his life at the dreadful sight.

"Here I am," called a steady voice from behind him. "Here I am."

"Run! Get a dry branch and light it, and then come here to me," shouted Heracles, giving ground again before the forest of heads, for he dared not let the poisonous fangs come too near. "Bring fire to lay across each head as I crush it. We will sear it well and see if it will grow again."

Iolaus tore for the thicket, but he had to light the whole grove to get enough fiery branches. All this took time, and in the meanwhile Heracles still battered vainly at the mass of heads. Every time he crushed one, two grew up in its place, but the Hydra shrank a little from his blows and he could keep it back for a while.

Iolaus rushed up the slope to Heracles with a great branch in his hand which flared up as he came. He was only just in time, for already Heracles' foot was caught fast in the Hydra's coils and the poisonous fangs were darting at his face. But as the hero struck out again, Iolaus with utter fearlessness darted in and laid the burning branch across the crushed and bleeding head. There was a fierce hissing, and the whole Hydra recoiled. At that Heracles wrenched his foot loose and struck again. Once more Iolaus darted in and laid his branch across the shattered neck. So they fought the Hydra together, Heracles dealing the blows and the boy dashing boldly within reach of the poisonous fangs to lay his burning branch across each wound. Since at the touch of the fire, the heads did not grow again, after long hours they were victorious together against all but the immortal head, which could not die. Finally Heracles cut it off and buried it, still struggling, under a mighty rock. Then he and Iolaus looked down at the monstrous beast.

The Hydra lay there in a huddled tangle of snaky heads, while the coils of its vast body trailed limply over the ground. All around the bare, poisoned earth was torn up by the struggle. Great furrows, blackened branches, and traces of blood were everywhere. The hero looked at it for a moment, weary but triumphant; then taking out his arrows he plunged them in the poisonous blood of the beast. He put them back in his quiver, fastening them in very carefully. He laid his hand on Iolaus' shoulder and they went down together to look for the horses. Heracles carried the deadly arrows at his back, but long years after, he was to regret that he had poisoned them.

3. Third and Fourth Labors

Eurystheus was disappointed when Heracles came back alive, but at least he got some satisfaction out of saying that, as Heracles had had help from Iolaus, this labor could not count among the ten. Heracles was forced to submit to this much against his will, and he again presented himself ready to do whatever King Eurystheus should command him. This time Eurystheus had rather run out of ideas. He would have liked to find something dangerous, but he could only think of something difficult. So he ordered him to capture a beautiful deer called the Cerynean Hind. While Heracles performed this labor, which took him a full year, King Eurystheus settled down to think of something really dangerous for next time.

The hind that Heracles was to fetch was a beautiful animal with golden horns, the favorite of Artemis. It ran wild on the wooded hills and shady valleys of Arcadia.

For a whole year Heracles hunted it through half the hills of Greece, wishing to take it alive, but though he spread the trails with nets, and though he himself was a tireless runner, he could never catch it. Often on moonlit nights he would see a glint of light on the pale gold horns, but instantly the hind was up and away, swifter even than other deer, leaping obstacles and avoiding nets as though the goddess Artemis were guiding it. At last Heracles saw that he could never catch the hind unharmed, so he wounded it with an arrow and thus captured it. Slinging it across his shoulders, he began the long journey back in triumph, but as he walked, there appeared to him in the woodland a young girl, fairer than human, with white tunic to the knee and bright hair caught back in a band of gold.

"How dared you harm my beautiful hind?" she demanded angrily.

Heracles knew he was in the presence of Artemis and he begged her to forgive him, pleading the command of Eurystheus and promising that after he had shown it to the king, the beast should be let go. Presently the goddess forgot her anger and smiled on him. So once more King Eurystheus, who had hoped to get Heracles into trouble, was disappointed.

For the fourth labor, Eurystheus now thought he had found something really dangerous, for he ordered Heracles to bring in the Erymanthian Boar alive. To overcome the savage beast at all seemed difficult to him, but to drag it all the way back to the city of Mycenae, still alive and struggling, was quite impossible, he thought. He rubbed his hands with particular satisfaction as he sent Heracles off on this errand, and for many a night he was joyful at the feastings as he drank his wine and pondered over his enemy's death.

On his way to the wild boar's lair, Heracles had to pass over many a wooded mountain, on one of which he came to the cave of a friendly centaur and went in to spend the night. Pholus was a simple creature, almost a savage. He ranged the wild forest with others of his

tribe, and they fed on nuts and acorns and the wild
beasts that they hunted. He was a man to the waist with
wild hair, shaggy chest, and great red beard. Below that
he had the body of a rough wild horse so that he could
tear clattering through the forest, club in hand, like
horse and huntsman all in one.

He received Heracles kindly, offered him a bed of
dried leaves and a seat by his smoky fire, and even remembered to put on some meat to roast for him, though
he himself preferred it raw. It was rather black on the
outside and rather red in the middle, but Heracles
thanked him and praised it and fell to eating heartily.
All was going very well when Heracles asked for wine.
Pholus' wide blue eyes looked a little puzzled, then he
glanced round the dark cave, put his finger to his lips,
and bent forward.

"Sh! Yes, I have some wine," he said in a low, hoarse
rumble, "a big pot of it. Oh, quite a lot. It's buried at the
back of the cave, but do you think I ought . . . ?"

"Why not?" asked Heracles half amused.

"Well, I've had it a long time, you see. It never has
been opened. And then there are the others. It really
belongs to us all. But you know a centaur can't drink
wine. It maddens him. They really oughtn't to have it,
so we never opened it."

"All the more reason to open it now," said Heracles
cheerfully. "I'll drink your wine for you and solve your
problem."

"Yes, but the others . . . ," said Pholus doubtfully.

"They'll smell it if it's opened, and they'll be furious . . . raging. Because if we ever did open it, we all ought to have a taste, you see."

"Smell it? Nonsense," said Heracles, for he was a man, not a wild beast, and he had no idea how keen the scent of beasts can be.

Pholus looked doubtful still, but he went and fetched the wine and watched while Heracles tasted it and pronounced it very good. But sure enough, just as Heracles was pouring himself a second cup, there was a clamor of angry shouts, a crashing and clattering of hoofs, and a whole band of centaurs came tearing up the hill brandishing sticks and stones and torches and anything that they could find. They were yelling and prancing about, their tails and long beards streaming in the wind, and shouting to Pholus that he was a thief and he should come out and be torn to pieces.

Heracles went to reason with them, but they were quite mad with rage and fell on him in a body, kicking and striking with all their strength. He jumped quickly behind a rock and took out his arrows. Then began a terrible slaughter, as centaur after centaur was stretched dead on the ground. The aim of the hero was deadly, and his arrows had been dipped in the Hydra's venom, so that even a scratch meant death. At last the few remaining centaurs could face no more and fled with wild yells into the forest. Then Heracles, searching for his arrows in the grass among the slain, came upon the old, wise Cheiron, tutor of Jason and Achilles and many famous heroes, who lay groaning from a wound in his knee. Cheiron was not a wild animal like the other centaurs; he was a kind, wise old man. He had come up late to the battle, hoping to be able to calm the others down, but he had been caught in the confusion and then struck by an arrow before Heracles knew he was there. Now he lay in agony, for though the poison burned like fire in his veins, he had the gift of immortality and could not die. Heracles ran to help him, applied salves to his wound, and did everything he could, but all in vain. At last Cheiron prayed to Zeus to take his immortality. Zeus had pity on him and did so, that the old centaur might die.

Heracles sorrowed for Cheiron and buried him with honor, but meanwhile poor, simple Pholus took up an arrow, marveling that such a little scratch could cause sudden death. He rattled it, sniffed it, and turned it over every way in his hands, shaking his head in slow puzzlement to find it so small and harmless. Presently he dropped it. It fell on his foot and in a second the poison passed into his veins. Heracles buried his second friend and set out sorrowing. This was the first time that he regretted poisoning his arrows; he was to regret it again.

Heracles then sought out the Erymanthian Boar in its lair and attacked it with spear and club till it fled before him. He drove it up the mountainside until he forced it into a deep snowdrift where it plunged till it was quite exhausted. He picked the brute up, slung it over his back upside down, and carried it, struggling, and gnashing its great tusks, all the way back to Mycenae.

Presently King Eurystheus got the news that Heracles was coming. He went up to the walls of Mycenae and actually saw him, bent under the weight of the vast, black, savage monster, which even from a distance was plainly very much alive. It began to dawn on King Eurystheus that this time he had been a bit too clever. Heracles was going to put that dreadful beast down right in front of him. It was going to tear like a thunderbolt straight at the nearest man, and he would certainly be the nearest man. King Eurystheus went deadly pale, and he raced back to his palace as fast as his trembling legs would carry him. But he wasn't safe there. Already he could hear the shouts and cheering as Heracles came through the city gate. In another minute or two he would be at the palace steps. Eurystheus tore through the great hall down into the cool, dark storage room at the back. There his eye fell on the huge water jars, half buried in the ground, which slaves filled every morning before the sun got hot. One of them was already empty. Happy thought! King Eurystheus clambered over the edge, slid into the cool, slimy inside, and pulled the lid over him with a bang. There they found him some hours later, still white and terrified, so that even his own servants had to smile. They could not resist teasing him with the announcement that Heracles was looking for him to present him with his boar.

4. Fifth, Sixth, and Seventh Labors

King Eurystheus had made himself ridiculous, and now he was even angrier than before. The first thing he did was to make a rule that in the future Heracles should deliver his prizes to the officials at the city gate and stay outside himself. All the same he was at a loss for a fifth labor, since he could not think of anything which would be dangerous to the man who could bring home alive on his shoulders the Erymanthian Boar. This time he simply determined to be insulting, and he told Heracles to go and clean out the stables of King Augeas in a single day.

Heracles was unable to refuse this command, but he thought he would get the better of Eurystheus none the less. His first move was to go to King Augeas and, without revealing that he had been commanded to do it, offer to clean out his stables single-handed for a great reward. King Augeas could hardly believe his ears. He was certain the task could not be done, and therefore he was willing to promise anything. The two made a bargain, and then Heracles went off to look over the stables for himself.

The herds of Augeas pastured around two rivers, and his stables were built where these flowed together. There were pens for sheep and pens for cattle, many pens for each because Augeas had countless herds. Heracles stood by them in the evening and watched the beasts come home. First were the sheep in enormous flocks with men behind them and dogs running hither and thither on either side. The whole meadow was covered with huddled, fleecy backs, and their baaing filled the air. Then came the cattle, herd on lowing herd, till the ground around the stables was all churned into mud. With the cows went three hundred white bulls and two hundred red ones. Twelve more which were sacred to the sun shone snowy and glistening amid the others. A small army of herdsmen fastened wooden guards about the feet of the cows that were to be milked, another group let the calves in to their mothers, some milked or carried pails. Everywhere lowing and bleating arose upon the evening air.

Augeas walked among his herdsmen, delighting in the bustle of it all. Many as were his cattle, he knew them all and would stop to talk over with his herdsmen how his favorites did. Heracles went with the king, marking the vast cattle pens and the incredible quantities of dung that were accumulating there. Now he could readily see that it was quite impossible for one man to carry it all out, but yet as he looked at the low-lying plain and the rivers running through it, a trick came into his mind which would outwit both King Augeas and King Eurystheus. For not only would it clear the Augean stables in a single day, but it would not force Heracles to degrade himself by lifting a single basket of dung.

Early in the morning Heracles was out by the stables, watching the herds depart. As soon as they were gone, he started digging a great ditch from the beds of the two rivers to the place where the stables lay. Then working with might and main he dammed the streams, lifting up huge logs single-handed and using vast rocks that no one else could carry. By midday the water was overflowing its banks and beginning to trickle into the ditch. An hour later it was flowing in a torrent into the stables of Augeas and clear across them, back into the stream bed lower down. In a few hours the rush of water had rolled all the dirt away. Heracles knocked down his own dams and blocked up his trenches, and by the time the herds came home at sunset, their whole yard was clean.

Augeas was furious. He had never intended to pay Heracles. It had never occurred to him that the question of payment would arise. Moreover, somebody had just told him that Heracles would have cleaned his stables for nothing, since Eurystheus had ordered him to. Augeas tried to deny his promise, and when witnesses agreed he had made it, he openly refused to keep it. He forced both Heracles and his own son, who supported the hero, to leave his kingdom. For his part, Eurystheus took the view that King Augeas owed Heracles payment, and he refused to count this labor as one of the ten.

The sixth task given to Heracles was to chase away the birds which infested the Stymphalian lake. These were a colony of the birds of Ares with which Jason and the Argonauts had fought. They had great claws of shining brass, sharp curving beaks, and brazen feathers which they could let fall spinning through the air from an immense height and which came down sharp end

foremost with the force of arrows. They preyed on all
living things within their reach, killing and carrying off
lambs and calves, and even young children. No man
had been able to shoot with force enough to hurt them,
but now Heracles took his bow, which none but he
could bend, and his arrows, from which a scratch
meant death, to see what he could do against these
fierce creatures.

At first sight it looked as though his task might be
difficult, for the birds were nesting among the reeds at
the end of the land, and it was hard to come at them or
to see how many there were. Heracles took a great,
brazen shield with which to cover himself from the
deadly feathers and huge brazen cymbals with which to
make a noise. Then, planting himself on a rocky headland which overlooked the lake, he clashed and clanged
with all his might till the birds flew up in great flocks
from the reedy marsh below. Then, protected by his
shield, he aimed his arrows and shot them down one by
one. The distant hills re-echoed with the clang of the
falling feathers and the harsh cries of the angry birds.
They darkened the sky over him like a cloud, and the
bolts fell thick as rain. But still the hero crouched safe
beneath his shield and, as he got a chance, loosed his arrows that never missed their mark. At last the
remaining birds wheeled round and fled away to the island of Ares far out in the unexplored sea, and the lake
of Stymphalus was deserted.

When Heracles returned from the Stymphalian lake,

Eurystheus, as a favor to King Minos, sent him off to Crete for his seventh labor. His task there was to capture the Cretan bull.

King Minos with his great sea empire was especially devoted to Poseidon. Many times he had sacrificed to the god, yet still he felt that he had paid him insufficient honor. For the great procession he at last planned, none of his possessions seemed a glorious enough offering. He went down to the sea, therefore, and prayed to Poseidon himself to send something more perfect than had ever yet been seen that men might talk of Poseidon's festival for generations to come. The great waves crashed on the beach in answer to his prayer, and from the foam there sprang up to the land a snow-white bull.

It was the most marvelous bull that anyone had yet beheld. Even the herds of Augeas held no such bull as this. It was huge, taller by two handbreadths than the largest of its kind. Its hair was white and curly, dazzling in the sun. Its horns were silvery as the water whence it had sprung, and its great, mild eyes were the deep blue of the sea.

King Minos had vast herds and was proud of them, but he had never seen such a bull as this. He thought of the snow-white cattle he could breed from it. He remembered his promise to Poseidon to slaughter this beast, and his heart was torn. Then the beautiful animal came up and nuzzled at his shoulder. He put an arm around its neck and felt the great, soft coat. He touched the silvery horns, and he simply could not bear to kill it. The festival took place next day with a lesser bull walking in the procession. But the occasion was remembered none the less, for at the very moment of the sacrifice, men came tearing up to Minos disheveled and gasping.

"The bull!" they panted, "the bull!" And for a moment that was all that they could say.

"How dare you disturb the sacrifice?" asked Minos angrily. "The bull can wait."

"It is the bull from the sea," said one who had got his breath a little. "Suddenly he went mad. As we were guarding the cattle, he went mad and came down upon us. Six men are dead, King Minos, and all your cattle are scattered. For the rest of us, we fled as best we could and left him bellowing and gouging at the grass in savage fury on an empty plain."

From that time until Heracles' arrival, the bull roamed the island, and no man's life was safe. Heracles could hardly persuade men to guide him to a grassy meadow where the bull was often seen. However, he faced the creature there at last and stood to await its charge. When it came, he stepped lightly to one side. Then he seized the animal by a silvery horn and twisted by main strength until the bull was forced to turn towards him. Then he grasped both horns and twisted again until it bellowed with pain and sank to its knees. For a long time it sought to toss its head and shake the hero off, or to lunge forward and impale him. At last, however, it saw that it had met its master and turned to

the hero as gently as it had turned to Minos when it first came out of the sea. Heracles took the bull back to Eurystheus, but he did not give him to the king. He merely showed him at Mycenae and then let him go.

5. Eighth, Ninth, and Tenth Labors

The eighth labor that Eurystheus gave to Heracles was to fetch the mares of Diomede. To the north of Greece lay the savage land of Thrace. It was a great country for horses and war chariots, but the mares of King Diomede were the fiercest and swiftest of them all. No man but their driver could be trusted with them, and there were rumors too that Diomede fed them on human flesh.

Heracles found that this horrible tale was perfectly true as he burst into the stables by main force in spite of the resistance of the grooms. Remains of the dreadful food were still in the mangers, and the mares were chained and hobbled to prevent them from killing the grooms. They turned on him with bared teeth as he broke the links that held them to the manger, but he seized each one by the mane and forced their heads apart. Then he led them out still shackled and trying their best to plunge and rear, but helpless in the grip of Heracles. The stable hands, who had felt his strength when they tried to prevent him from entering, dared not raise hand against him, but stood by and watched him go. Heracles might have got off unmolested if the huge Diomede had not made after him. With a roar of rage he rushed at Heracles, who seized him round the waist and hurled him headlong. Unfortunately he fell at the feet of his own mares, and that was the end of him.

Heracles gave these mares as a present to Eurystheus. He must have thought that such a gift would embarrass the cowardly king. Sure enough, after not very long they burst out of their stables and escaped. But they did no harm, for they went to the woods of Mount Olympus, and there wild beasts devoured them.

By now Eurystheus had despaired of destroying Heracles. All he could think of was to get him away for a good, long time. For the ninth labor he sent him to fetch the girdle of Hippolyte, who was queen of the far distant Amazons.

The Amazons were a nation of women, great archers and fighters. They visited their husbands in another country and they sent their male children there, but they reared the females themselves and taught them how to fight so fiercely that all the neighboring lands were afraid of them. The shimmering belt of Hippolyte, which was the token of her authority, had been given her by Ares. Eurystheus hoped that to fight with a whole nation for the precious object would be beyond even Heracles' powers.

For this ninth labor Heracles needed a ship and a crew of warriors, and he sent out messages to all the lands of Greece for volunteers. Soon men came flocking to join him as eagerly as they had come to sail with Jason on the *Argo*. Heracles set forth with his comrades and sailed across the sea to the northeast along the path the Argonauts had taken. He and his friends had many adventures on the way, for the journey was long and as perilous as Eurystheus had hoped. As always, however, everything Heracles did only served to increase his reputation, so that when he came to the land of the Amazons, it seemed at first as though he were going to have no trouble at all. For the queen of the warrior Amazons loved bravery, whether in man or woman, and when she heard of Heracles' arrival, she came in person down to his ship to visit him. Heracles greeted her royally and told her why he had come. And at that the queen laughed and gave him the girdle, saying: "Ares himself gave me this girdle because, though a woman, my whole soul is set on deeds of daring and heroism in war. With what better gift could I honor the hero whom all Greece declares the greatest of mankind?"

Heracles thanked the queen for her gift, and the two talked together in friendship, telling each other stories of the great deeds they had seen and done. As they sat together, a mob of yelling Amazons came sweeping down onto the beach. The queen's guard of honor, who had escorted her to the shore, had seen her take off the flashing belt and hand it to Heracles as she stood on the deck of the ship. Instantly the word went around among them that the queen was made a prisoner. Some stayed to watch and wait while a group sped off to the city to arouse the others. Now they all came tearing down like a swarm of angry bees. Some rained arrows on the ship from behind the sand dunes; others swam out through the shallow water and swarmed up the anchor ropes. The sea was alive with them. They caught at the oar-holes and pulled themselves over the side. They leaped on the deck, fierce and nimble as tigers. They fell on the men like furies, without thought for their own lives.

There was no chance to explain. One moment all was peaceful; in the next there was utter confusion. The men grabbed their own weapons and resisted as best they could. In the end it was the presence of Heracles that turned the scale. Outnumbered though his men were, with his irresistible strength on their side they had the advantage. He seemed all over the deck at once, and with every blow an Amazon lay dead. At last the remainder saw they were defeated and fled in dismay, leaving the deck strewn with corpses, among which lay the body of Hippolyte. In the confusion the queen herself, the innocent cause of the battle, had been killed. Heracles sailed away with the girdle and brought it to Eurystheus, but he sorrowed for the death of the brave queen who had given him her friendship.

Having sent Heracles to the east to face the dangers there, Eurystheus now determined to send him to the west. Accordingly he ordered him for the tenth labor to fetch the cattle of Geryon from Gadira, which is now the Spanish port of Cadiz. Geryon was a vast monster who was one man from the waist down but three from the waist up. He had three heads and six arms, while his strength was also that of three, so that he was famed to be the strongest of mankind. As for Gadira, it was out on the great ocean which was the border of the known world. Far as he had been at the commands of Eurystheus, Heracles had never been as far as this.

This time Heracles took ship for Crete and thence to Egypt and traveled all across North Africa to the strait which divides it from Spain. On the way there he performed great feats wherever he went. Men said he cleared Crete of wild beasts, conquered Egypt, killed all the wild beasts which infested North Africa, and came at last to the narrow sea which divides North Africa from Spain. Here Heracles stood on the very edge of the world, and to commemorate his journey he set up two immense rocks, one on each side of the strait. There the hills stand to this day on either side of the seaway between the Mediterranean and the Atlantic. The most famous of them is now named Gibraltar, but the Greeks called both the Pillars of Heracles.

From the Pillars of Heracles, the hero embarked on the vast Atlantic ocean which the Greeks called part of the River of Ocean that they thought ran round the edge of the world. Some say that the sun god himself gave him a golden cup, huge as a boat, and that he set out in that on the deep, mysterious sea. For he bent his bow at the sun in anger at the heat of the African shore, and the sun god laughed at his daring and aided him. Then Oceanus himself, on whose River the hero was journeying, was angry at the impertinence of the mortal who dared sail his great waters. He raised a huge storm, and the magic cup rocked wildly amid the boiling spray. At last Heracles saw the distant figure of old Oceanus, his long white beard streaming over the waters, and aimed an arrow at him. Then Oceanus too laughed and allowed him to proceed.

Heracles landed close by Gadira and came on the red cattle of Geryon grazing in a green meadow. Immediately he was attacked by Geryon's great two-headed dog, which came at him snarling and leaped straight for his throat. With a single blow of his club Heracles laid the monster low and turned to face Geryon's savage herdsman, who was also attacking him. He too fell before Heracles' club, and then the hero herded the cattle together, with some difficulty for they were very wild, and started to drive them off. At that up came the monster Geryon, striding along with a tread that shook the ground. His three heads bristled with rage, his three mouths roared out threats, and each of his six arms brandished a mighty club. Eurystheus had sent Heracles out hoping that here at last was a stronger man in whom he would meet his match. Geryon certainly looked dangerous, but for once Heracles did not stop to wrestle with him. Instead he laid him low with a deadly arrow, drove the herd into his magic cup, and set out with them for the Pillars of Heracles. From there, however, he drove the cattle all the way back by land, up through Spain, round the sea to Italy, and thence overland to Greece. Once people tried to steal the cattle.

Once they were scattered in the mountains by a plague of stinging flies. One bull swam across the straits to Sicily, and Heracles had to go over and bring it back. Some he lost completely. Nevertheless he brought most of the herd safely back and gave it to King Eurystheus.

6. Eleventh and Twelfth Labors

The tenth labor was completed by the end of eight years, the length of time Heracles' service to King Eurystheus was supposed to take. But now Eurystheus claimed two more labors from him in place of the Lernaean Hydra and the Augean stables. These last two Heracles was bound to perform also, and Eurystheus saw to it that they were labors which should take him a long time.

The first of these tasks, the eleventh labor, was to fetch the apples of the Hesperides. Long ago at the wedding of Zeus and Hera, all things had brought presents to the bride. The gift of Earth had been trees with golden apples, shining like stars but sweet and scented as other apples are. They were a marvel among all fruits, the fairest that had ever been seen.

When the goddess saw these, she loved them more than all her other gifts, and had them planted in the garden of the gods. This was a lovely garden full of green meadows and golden daffodils. In it grew all the flowers that the gods delight in: roses, violets, narcissus, and many others, all larger and fairer than anywhere else on earth. There were tall, green trees, arbors of trailing vines, white blossoming pear trees, dark cherries, and every kind of fruit. The nymphs who dwelt by its bubbling streams were called Hesperides, and since they cared for the garden, it was often called the Garden of the Hesperides.

But delightful as was the garden, nothing in it had ever yet been seen so fair as the golden apples of Hera. Presently, therefore, Hera sent a dragon there to help the nymphs guard the treasure, which Eurystheus now ordered Heracles to steal.

It happened that while men knew about this garden, the apples, and the watching dragon, no one knew certainly where the garden was to be found, for it was a secret retreat for the pleasure of the gods into which men might not come. Heracles had to set forth, he knew not whither, asking all he came upon if they had heard of the garden. At last he came to the river Eridanus, which is now called the Po. There he saw the white river nymphs in their silvery garments playing on the broad, blue stream, and he called to them, saying, "Tell me, daughters of Zeus, where lies the Garden of the Hesperides?"

The river nymphs ceased their rippling laughter and looked at him suspiciously, ready to dart away like fish into the bottom of the stream. But the eldest of the nymphs recognized the hero by his club and lionskin and answered him fearlessly.

"We only know that we do not pass that garden as we ride down our hurrying stream from the mountains to the sea. Ask the wise god Nereus, for he is very old, and the ocean, touching all lands, beholds many things. He knows the garden if you can make him tell."

"But how shall I find Nereus?" Heracles answered her. "I cannot pursue a sea god into the ocean's depths. How shall I make him tell?"

"There is a little cove," said the eldest nymph, "which we see when we swim out into the ocean where the fresh water mingles with the salt. There old Nereus comes when the tide is low to sleep on a cushion of seaweed in the bright rays of the sun. Hide there and watch him; then steal up and seize him while he sleeps. When he wakes and finds you have caught him, he will change himself into many different shapes, since he is as hard to grasp as water. Yet hold him fast, for when at last he sees that he is captured, he will tell you all you wish." She was gone with her sisters in a silvery flash, and only a ripple lingered on the surface of the stream.

Down near the mouth of the river Heracles found the rocky cove, and while the tide was yet high he hid himself there to wait the slow hours till it went down. At last when the wet rocks and little pools lay uncovered in the sun, he saw snow-white sea gulls wheeling and turning over a great wave coming in from the sea. The wave reared up and broke in a green wall, and out of the foam rose a little, bent old man. Water dripped from his fingers and the ends of his long, white hair. Shells and seaweed hung in his locks; green ooze covered his garments. He came puffing slowly up between the rocks, but his sea-blue eyes were bright and keen.

At length he came to a low, flat rock, sloping gently

from the edge of a little pool. There he laid himself down on the seaweed cushion, and the gulls flew silently round him for fear of disturbing him. Then he slept, his feet half in clear water, while the sea anemones waved beneath them and the crabs and starfish climbed idly around. Presently he snorted, like a great old sea lion, until the whole cove resounded with his breathing. A smell of fish arose in the warm air.

Heracles crept from his hiding and seized the old man in his mighty arms. Quick as a flash the blue eyes opened, the old limbs twitched, and in a moment the god was gone and Heracles found himself plunged to the shoulders in a raging fire. For a second his grip relaxed, and then, for the fire did not burn, he clutched more tightly than ever at what he could feel, though he did not see. The form changed under his hands to a leaping stag, and he caught the animal to his breast just as it was jumping free. It shrank in his arms to a screaming seagull which pecked at his eyes and struggled to get loose. He crushed it tight against him, and in the instant it was a raging lion. He seized it by the neck and held it at arm's length away from him, but it changed to water and ran through his fingers in the twinkling of an eye. He hurled himself at the little pool, falling headlong on top of it, and it became a coiling snake, wriggling from underneath. This he seized by the neck and squeezed savagely, and with that the god gave in, and Heracles found himself lying on top of the old man himself with his fingers on his throat.

Then old Nereus, seeing that there was no escape,

gave Heracles the answer he wished to know. "Go to
the mountains of Atlas," he said, "where that giant
stands, supporting on his shoulders the blue bowl of the
sky. Ask him about the Hesperides, for they are his
daughters, and at his bidding they will give the apples
to you."

Heracles released the sea god and set out once more.
At the end of his journey he came to the mighty giant,
standing bowed beneath the great weight of the sky.

"Yes, I know the garden," Atlas answered the hero,
"but you can never enter there. It is the special garden
of the gods themselves; no mortal man has ever set foot
in it. Do but hold up the weight of the sky for me, and I
will fetch the apples that Eurystheus asks of you."

Heracles bowed his back to receive the monstrous
weight, and the giant slipped away from under it and
set out for the Hesperides. It seemed a long wait to
Heracles. Even his mighty muscles were cracking beneath the strain when at length the giant returned with
three of the gleaming apples in his hand. "Stay here," he
said happily to the hero. "For many ages I have
cramped my muscles beneath this load. Now it is your
turn. I will take the apples to Eurystheus and tell him
you sent them."

Heracles glanced at Atlas in dismay, but the giant
was quite in earnest. Heracles was dreadfully afraid
that he would never be released from his burden, but he
thought of a trick, and pretending willingness, he said:
"It is indeed my turn, and I should be glad to bear the
burden for you for a little while. Why should I run

across the earth at the commands of King Eurystheus?
Take him the apples and tell him I cannot come. Never-
theless, before you go, take the weight for a little, while
I fold my lionskin into a pad for my shoulders."

The simple-minded giant took up the burden again
and released Heracles, who did not stay to help him
further. He took the apples and at once set off for
Greece.

This was the eleventh labor of Heracles, and for the
twelfth Eurystheus thought of the most terrible thing of
all. He bade Heracles go down into the land of the dead
and bring up Cerberus, the three-headed dog who
watches at Hades' gate. He hoped, of course, that Heracles would be lost forever, as Theseus had been lost —
that the powers of the underworld would be strong
enough to keep him imprisoned. But Heracles simply
shouldered his club and made off down the long, dark,
winding road to the grey banks of the Styx and the
shadowy towers which guard the lands of the dead. He
took no gifts for the ferryman as Psyche had, nor had
he the magic voice of Orpheus to move the listening
ghosts to tears. Yet he strode through the waiting
shades unafraid and faced old Charon with such boldness that the grim, red-eyed ferryman shrank from him
and let him stride unmolested into his muddy barge.
Thus Heracles crossed the wailing river, while the barge
sank low in the water at the weight of a living man.

At the gate of Hades sat the three-headed dog, its
eyes as huge as saucers and its grinning teeth as fierce

as those of a great lion. When it saw the huge hero advancing on him in the midst of the pale throngs of ghosts, the snarling died away in its three throats and it crouched before him. For the moment Heracles passed it by and came through the gates into Hades' house. There from the dark anteroom came a cry, and Heracles saw his friend Theseus imprisoned in a huge chair of stone. Theseus had come down safely to Hades, living man though he was, but when he came to the house of Hades he sat down when invited on this magic chair. Then the chair held him fast, and for all his strength he might have sat there forever if Heracles had not burst his bonds for him.

Heracles strode into the dark hall where grey Hades sat beside the pale Persephone, and asked them if he might carry Cerberus up to the daylight. He did not do this of his own will, he said, but by command of King Eurystheus, and when he had brought him the dog, he would let it go again.

The grave Hades nodded, and sad Persephone smiled on him, but neither said a word. Thereupon Heracles strode out to Cerberus and grasped him as he lay crouched in the shadow of the gate. At that the monster let out a deadly howl such as the underworld had never heard before, and the three dog's heads gnashed and tore at Heracles, while the serpent that was its tail wound round his limbs. But Heracles held him so tightly that the heads were half strangled and could not get a grip except on the lionskin which partly protected him. For all the pain, Heracles hung on, throttling harder, till the snarling died away into muffled growls and the jaws relaxed. Then he heaved the animal over his shoulder and carried him up, the three hideous heads lying limply by his own, and the huge length trailing behind him on the rocky ground.

The road was steep, yet his strength never failed. All the way up to the world he carried him, and staggered out into the light. He reeled across the plain to Mycenae, keeping his strangling grip on the beast, for he dared not for an instant let go. When he came to the city gate where he should show his prize, the judges fled in dismay before him, and he stalked through the gate unmolested and himself laid the hideous beast at King Eurystheus' feet.

Eurystheus was almost terrified out of his wits by Cerberus. He had never intended to see him at all, and only by the flight of his guards had he been exposed to him. Nevertheless he was forced to admit that Heracles' labors were fairly ended and could only revenge himself by driving the hero out of the city, telling him not to return.

7. The Death of Heracles

Heracles went back to Thebes, since Eurystheus would have none of him, and he wooed a certain princess, Iole, in marriage. Glorious as was the hero's fame, Iole's father refused him, since he remembered the fate of the Theban princess who had been Heracles' first wife.

After vainly striving for Iole, Heracles at last married a sister of Meleager, Deianira, who proved a noble wife to him. As he was journeying with her from her father's house to his own, they came to a flooded stream. Heracles waded across it, as the strength of the water meant nothing to him, but he asked the centaur, Nessus, who happened to be there, to carry Deianira across on his back.

The rough centaur agreed gladly, for the beauty of Deianira had made a great impression on his savage mind. As soon as she was on his back, he turned and made off with her, thinking to carry her away. Frightened Deianira cried aloud for rescue, and Heracles, fitting a poisoned arrow to the string, struck the centaur full in the chest. He fell to the ground dying in agony, and Heracles waded back across the water to fetch his bride. The girl was tender-hearted and unused to scenes of bloodshed. At the sight of Nessus' wound she forgot her fear and stooped over him to help if she could. Then the centaur in rage and agony spoke to her before Heracles came up.

"Take the blood from my wound," he gasped to her, "where the poison has clotted it, and make an ointment. Keep it by you always; it is a love charm. If ever Heracles forgets his love to you, smear this on a garment and have him put it on. Then his love will revive and be as it is now. Take it as my dying gift because you showed me pity." At that he died, and Deianira did as he had said.

Long years passed, and many were Heracles' adven-

tures. Often in rage he did wrong, but always he won great glory for his daring and for his desire to help mankind. At last, however, Heracles once more caught sight of Iole. Immediately his love for her was rekindled, so he made war on her land and carried her off, lost to all other thoughts.

When the news came to Deianira that Heracles had forgotten her, her sorrow was very great. She felt no anger against him but only wished to regain his love. Then she remembered the ointment she had got from Nessus years before, and she went to her treasure chest and took out a splendid robe. She took a handful of wool, smeared it in the ointment, and with it covered the robe as best she could, rubbing it in well. She gave the robe to a messenger, saying, "Take this robe to my husband and say to him, 'Deianira sends you this garment in token that she is your loving wife and prays that when next you make a sacrifice, you put it on.'" The wool with which she had smeared the robe was tossed out into the yard in the sun.

Some time later Deianira happened to cross the court and her eyes fell on this wool. To her horror she saw that it was all black and eaten away as though by acid. Then she understood the cunning of the centaur who had given her a deadly poison and persuaded her it was a love charm. She ran frantically to find a messenger and send Heracles a warning, but it was already too late.

Deianira's present came to Heracles as he was preparing a great sacrifice. The hero received it gladly, for he honored Deianira in spite of his infatuation for Iole, and he was relieved that she sent love instead of reproaches to him. Therefore he took the robe, for all that it was dark and evil-smelling, and immediately put it on. For a short time all seemed well, but after a while his body warmed the garment as the sun had warmed the little piece of wool in the courtyard of Deianira. Then the poison from his own arrow which was mingled with the centaur's blood began to work. Heracles burned as though with fire, and when he tried to tear the robe from him he could not. He screamed aloud, cursed poor Deianira, threw himself from side to side, broke trees, dashed himself against stones in his agony. No one of his servants dared approach him.

At last, however, even Heracles' great strength could bear the poison no more, and he lay helpless on the ground. Then he bade his servants make a huge pile of wood, lay him upon it, and let him perish in the flame. He wished to die in splendor as he had lived and to go to his death like a hero. So the servants made a great pyre for Heracles, and he burned in a mighty blaze upon a great mountain top. Poor, innocent Deianira hanged herself, since she could not bear to live after what she had done.

Thus died Heracles, the greatest hero that there ever was. The gods did not let his shade rest in the underworld where, in his living body, he had terrified Charon himself. For his great deeds they called him up to Olympus, gave him a heavenly body, and made him immortal like themselves. Thereafter Heracles dwelt in Olympus

as the god of strength, and Hebe, the fair-cheeked goddess of youth, became his bride. Henceforth the Greeks
thought of him chiefly as one who had proved that
by the greatness of his deeds a man can even become
divine.

A List of PROPER NAMES and
PRONUNCIATION GUIDE

A-chil'-les
A-cris'-i-os
Ac-tae'-on
Ad-me'-tus
A-do'-nis
Ae-e'-tes
Ae-ge'-an sea
Ae'-ge-us
Ae'-son
Ae'-thra
Al-ces'-tis
Alc-me'-na
Al-thae'-a
Am'-a-zons
Am-phi'-try-on
An-drom'-e-da
An-tei'-a
Aph-ro-di'-te
A-pol'-lo
A-rach'-ne
A'-res
Ar'-go
Ar-go-naut'
Ar'-gos

A-ri-ad'-ne
Ar'-tem-is
At-a-lan'-ta
Ath'-a-mas
Ath-e'-ne
Ath'-ens
At'-las
At'-tic-a
Au'-ge-as

Bab'-y-lon
Bac-chan'-tes
Bac'-chus
Bau'-cis
Bel-ler'-o-phon
Bos'-phor-os

Cal'-y-don
Cas-si-o-pei'-a
Ce'-crops
Ce'-phe-us
Cer-y-ne'-an hind
Chal'-y-bes
Cha'-ron
Cheir'-on
Chi-me'-ra

Cly'-me-ne
Cly'-tie
Cnos'-sos
Col'-chis
Cor'-inth
Cre'-on
Crete
Cre'-the-us
Crom'-my-on
Cu'-pid

Dae'-da-lus
Dan'-a-e
Daph'-ne
De-i-an-i'-ra
De'-los
Del'-phi
De-me'-ter
De-mo'-pho-on
Deu-ca'-li-on
Dic'-tys
Di'-o-mede
Di-o-ny'-sus

E'-cho
E-lys'-i-um
En-dym'-i-on
E'-os
E-pa'-phos
Ep-i-me'-theus
E-rid-a'-nus
E'-ros
Er-y-man'-thi-an boar
Eu-phra'-tes
Eu-ryd'-i-ce
Eu-rys'-theus

Ga-di'-ra
Ga-la-te'-a
Gan'-y-mede
Ge'-ry-on
Gor'-gons

Ha'-des
Har'-pies
He'-be
Hec'-a-te
Hel'-le
Hel'-les-pont
Her'-a-cles
Her'-mes
Hes-per'-i-des
Hip-pol'-y-te
Hip-po'-men-es
Hy-a-cin'-thus

Ic'-a-rus
I'-no
I-ob'-a-tes
I-o-la'-us
I-ol'-cos
I'-o-le
Iph'-i-cles
I'-ris
Ix-i'-on

Ja'-son

Kro'-nos

La-ris'-sa
Ler-nae'-an hy'-dra
Le'-to
Lib'-y-a
Ly'-ci-a

Mai'-a
Mar'-a-thon
Me-de'-a
Me-du'-sa
Me-le-a'-ger
Met-a-nei''-ra
Mi'-das
Mi'-nos
Min'-o-taur
Mu'-ses

Nar-cis'-sus
Na'-xos
Ne-me'-an lion
Ne'-phe-le
Ne'-re-us
Nes'-sus
Nin'-us
Ni'-o-be

O-ce'-an-us
Oe'-neus
Oe-no'-ne
O-lym'-pus
Or'-pheus

Pan
Pan-do'-ra
Par-nas'-sus
Par'-then-on
Peg'-a-sus
Pe'-li-as
Pen'-theus
Per-seph'-o-ne
Per'-seus
Pha'-e-thon
Phe'-rae

Phi-le'-mon
Phoe'-bus
Pho'-lus
Phor'-ci-des
Phri'-xus
Phryg'-i-a
Pol-y-dec'-tes
Po-sei'-don
Pro-crus'-tes
Proi'-tos
Pro-me'-theus
Psy'-che
Pyg-ma'-li-on
Pyr'-a-mus
Pyr'-rha

Sa'-tyrs
Sci'-ron
Scy'-ros
Sem'-e-le
Si-le'-nus
Si'-nis
Sis'-y-phus
So'-ly-mi
Stym-pha'-li-an lake
Styx

Tan'-ta-lus
Ten'-a-ros
Thebes
The'-se-us
Thes'-sa-ly
This'-be
Ti-tho'-nus
Tmo'-lus
Troe-zen'